"Unflinching h
small but telli a
quiet dark ge out
filled with a r help
but feel in yo
moment afte
– Eris Young,

"A queer moral vision wrapped in the skin of a woodsy, witchy parable of everyday monstrosity and of just how far normalcy will go to protect itself."
– Jeanne Thornton, author of *Summer Fun*

"Jesse's family moved to Narrowbrook to get away from the darkness and dangers of the city, but not everything in Narrowbrook is as safe as it might seem. It is a town haunted by gossip and something sinister is happening just beneath the surface. *The False Sister* is a dark, queer modern folk fable about the violence perpetrated against those who are perceived as different. With great clarity and precision Briar Ripley Page summons the quiet horror of small town adolescence, and the fear we feel growing up not fully understanding ourselves, or the world around us. Perfect for fans of Eric LaRocca, Angela Carter, and *The X-Files*."
– Alex Thornber, *Book Talk*

"Imagine if Shirley Jackson was a little imp who lived in a hole in a tree."
– Gretchen Felker-Martin, author of *Manhunt*

Praise for Briar Ripley Page's writing:

"Page's talent for transporting readers into tableaus of awe inspiring beauty and chaotic torrents of gut-wrenching disgust are in full force in this tender and brutally honest exploration of the human condition."
– Eve Harms, author of *Transmuted*, reviewing *Corrupted Vessels*

"[...] as a fundamentally queer story, is much more than the varied genders and sexualities of its cast, because it aligns with the promise of a particular approach to queerness: what things are called is not important, because labels are, at best, approximations. What matters instead is materiality, what happens, what people feel, how they act toward each other, and what they do, whether or not it's motivated by a belief that's verifiably true."
– June Martin, reviewing *Corrupted Vessels* for Heavy Feather Review

"The characters stay sympathetic and relatable, through the most brutal acts."
– I. Merey, author of *A+E 4ever*, reviewing *Corrupted Vessels*

Thank you!

A special thank you from the Knight Errant team to our supporters who backed our 2023 list campaign and made this another exciting year in books for our team and writers.

In no particular order we would like to thank our Generous Benefactor backers Argonaut Books, Caith, Frederick Rossero, Barry Norton, Sam Hirst and Charles Page for their support.

We would also like to thank Ian W. and Jamie Graham for their unprecedented generosity and support for the small arts. Thank you all! You, our readers, make these projects possible.

Published by Knight Errant Press CIC
Falkirk, Scotland
www.knighterrantpress.com

Design and typesetting by Nathaniel Kunitsky

ISBN (paperback): 978-1-9996713-7-2

eISBN (ebook): 978-1-916665-00-2

Printed and bound in Great Britain by Clays Ltd, Elcograf S.p.A

Knight Errant Press acknowledges support for this title from a Kickstarter campaign, which was partially funded by the Creative Scotland Forward Funds programme.

THE FALSE SISTER

by

Briar Ripley Page

Knight Errant Press

2023

CONTENT WARNING

Use of recreational substances; mention of recreational drugs and other pharmaceuticals; graphic violence and gore; blood; homophobia and transphobia (reference in context only); gaslighting; death; reference to poor mental health and self-harm; reference to murder.

For my parents and siblings. I am so lucky and grateful that you all support both my transition and my writing.

THE FALSE SISTER

by

Briar Ripley Page

1

Crys disappeared during the night of the summer solstice, when it was so humid it felt like God draped a damp, warm washcloth over the world. Or at least the town of Narrowbrook. Frogs sang through the sticky, firefly-spangled dark. Crys told Jesse long ago, and a library book confirmed it later, that fireflies only light themselves up to attract other fireflies for sex. Frogs sing for the same reason.

Jesse was almost twelve, and he wondered when and if his own animal instincts would wrest control of his behaviour and make him start doing things just to impress girls. Singing. Whatever the equivalent of a glowing butt was for humans. He had started to get boners, but so far they weren't for girls, or for any reason in particular that he could tell. He hoped he would never start gooning after pretty women, thinking that he was in love. He hoped he would be like his older sister. Sure, Crys had sex. She had boyfriends. But she never seemed to do anything to attract the boyfriends, and she never seemed to care that much when they went away. She was a proud loner, except for Jesse and her best friend Marcus the weed dealer. Then their parents moved them out of their city apartment and into the Narrowbrook house, and Crys only had Jesse. That was okay; Jesse only had Crys.

Except he didn't, really. That evening, he and Crys watched the late sunset on the Narrowbrook house's splintery back porch. They'd been doing that ever since it got warm out. They could talk, or not talk, and Crys might smoke a surreptitious cigarette. Their parents didn't bother them. It was a pocket of calm, looking out at the spiky black edge of the forest that bordered their yard. It was a pocket of calm until Crys tore through its lining with a few blunt, emphatic words: she told Jesse she was planning to run away soon.

"Why?" asked Jesse. Then, "Can I come, too?"

Crys exhaled with her teeth shut, making a snaky whistling noise. "Jesse. I'm sorry. No. I'll write, I promise! But you've gotta stay here. It's gonna be hard enough making it on my own without a kid in tow. Anyway, you actually seem to like Narrowbrook. And I'm the one who's in danger."

"How come you think you're in danger?" Jesse picked at a scab on his elbow.

"I've heard Mom and Dad talking. They're thinking of doing something to me. Sounds like they're planning to send me to a shrink again, drug me up. Maybe worse. A psych ward or one of those forced labour camps for troubled teens."

"They wouldn't do that! Would they? I mean, why now? You did way crazier stuff when we lived in the city."

"I guess." Crys' shaggy bangs had fallen over her eyes, and she stared intently at her dirty fingernails. The evening light gave her a ghostly glow. Jesse could see some of the individual blood vessels running through her raised hand. They blended in with the crosshatch of cuts and scars poking out from her sweatshirt sleeve.

"I mean, the problem is that I still do crazy stuff in Narrowbrook. They thought the move would calm me down, or make me normal. But it didn't, and people notice the crazy stuff even more here. They kept sending me home from school all through the spring semester. I got arrested for shoplifting fucking Ace bandages from the Rite Aid. These podunk cops are all bored as shit, Jesse. They'd probably have arrested me for jaywalking, too."

"Yeah," Jesse agreed. He wasn't sure if he thought shoplifting was wrong or not, but he admired his sister for being brave enough to do it. And he wasn't a fan of the cops.

"So Mom and Dad are at their wit's end, I guess. They think nothing they do is going to change me or fix me — and it won't — and the neighbours are gossiping about how they can't control me. I was always gonna leave when I turned eighteen, anyway, you know. It'll just have to happen a little early."

"Are shrinks really all that bad?"

"The one I saw in the city was. Don't even ask me to talk about him, Jess. And the drugs he gave me made me all shaky and nauseous. They didn't help anything. I couldn't sleep and I had to piss all the time."

"Maybe a different kind of medication could help, though. I was reading this article in one of Dad's magazines the other day, and—"

"Jesus Christ, Jesse, you're supposed to be on *my* side! How would you like it if they tried to give *you* pills?"

"I guess that would depend on what the pills did."

Crys glared at him and made like she was about to turn around and stomp back inside the house. "I'm not having this argument with you, Jesse. And you'd better not tell anyone I'm leaving."

"I won't," said Jesse softly. "Please stay for a little longer."

"Okay." Crys relented as quickly as she'd gotten upset. That didn't phase Jesse; he was used to her moods.

The bottom of the sky was a shimmering pool of red and hot pink. The top had begun to darken. No clouds. Crys' face was almost as pink as the sunset, but Jesse knew she wouldn't take her sweatshirt off. When she hugged him, she felt moist and bony and she didn't smell too good. Jesse held her tight anyway, for as long as she'd let him.

"I can't take you with me," Crys whispered in his ear, "but I'll write you. I promise. Postcards from the city, or any other city I travel to. I'll be fine. In a little over a year I'll be eighteen, and then I can even come back for a visit."

"Please, Crys, don't. We can talk to Mom and Dad! They're nice people, they won't make you go somewhere bad."

Crys laughed. "Of course they will. They're nice people, but I'm a terrible daughter. I'm the worst daughter in the world. I probably *ought* to be locked up. But I don't want to be. I gotta live free."

Now that he was almost about to be a man, Jesse had been trying hard not to cry anymore. He was usually pretty successful. Even with Crys talking about how she planned to abandon him and flee back to the city, he managed to keep his tears shut away behind his eyeballs. Their pressure gave him a headache, but his voice was steady when he told Crys that he loved her, and asked her one last time not to go.

"I love you too, Jess," she said into his hair. She squeezed him. She rocked him back and forth like he was a little kid. The porch creaked. The frogs sang. The sun vanished beneath the horizon.

She did not tell him she would stay, but she

did not say anything more about leaving, either.

Crys and Jesse went inside and brushed their teeth and retired to their separate bedrooms. Jesse to read a few more chapters of *The Hobbit* before falling asleep and Crys to do who knew what. Jesse heard the faint sound of Nirvana coming through the wall as he slipped from waking life to troubled dreams, and the even fainter sound of Crys' feet dancing on the bare floorboards. It didn't seem like she intended to run away that night, at least.

But Crys was gone in the morning. Jesse never saw her alive again.

2

Neither Jesse nor his parents wondered where Crys was at breakfast. She usually slept through it anyway.

Jesse's mom shut herself up in the backyard studio where she made pottery. Jesse's dad drove into town to work at his office. Jesse watched a half-hour of TV. The news people on TV were talking about some sports guy named O.J. Simpson who'd murdered his wife or something. Jesse figured it'd be a really big deal if he knew anything about football, or famous people. Or if he thought murders were interesting, like Marcus the weed dealer. Marcus had a T-shirt with a big bloody knife on the front and was always reading out loud from books about Charles Manson and Jack the Ripper.

Instead, Jesse got bored of hearing about O.J. and the dead lady named Nicole. They didn't mean anything to him. He turned the TV off and went back to his room. He read some. He made sure everything on the shelves was lined up just the way he liked it. The spines of the books all had to be at the same level. His seashell and rock collection was organised by colour and size, each object spaced one inch exactly from the objects flanking it on either side.

He glanced over at his clock radio. The glowing red dashes spelled out 12:30 p.m.

That meant he should probably make himself lunch, and see if Mom or Crys wanted any. But where *was* Crys? She was almost always awake by noon.

Jesse remembered the sunset. The sour smell of his sister's sweatshirt.

I'll write you. I promise.

He dashed out into the hall and pounded on Crys' bedroom door. Maybe his intuition was wrong.

"Crys!" he called. "Wake up!"

Silence.

"*Crystal*!" Crys hated her full name, even though their parents and some of her boyfriends never called her anything else. Getting her mad would get her attention if she was in one of her moody slumps. "Crystal, stop messing around! Open the door!"

More silence. It didn't feel like the silence of a person who wasn't speaking. It felt like the silence of a room with no one in it. Jesse's stomach felt tight and fluttery.

"Crystal, you fuckhead! Come on!" Jesse knocked on the door one last time, then tried the knob. It wasn't locked.

Crys' room looked the way it usually looked. Posters, postcards, drawings and images torn from magazines were taped all over the walls.

Her narrow, kid-size bed was unmade and there were crumbs on the sheets. Rumpled clothes, most of them grey or black or dark blue, sat in slumped piles all over the floor. It was impossible to tell which clothes were clean and which were dirty. Between the clothes piles were teetering stacks of books, records and tapes. Crys' record player was still wedged in its accustomed corner, but Jesse didn't see her Walkman anywhere. Despite Crys' belongings scattered everywhere, despite the smell of Crys that hung over everything, despite the faint indentation her head had left on her pillow, the room had an air of abandonment. Jesse felt more and more sure, with each careful step he took across the cluttered floor, that his sister had run away for good.

It was really hard to tell what, if anything, she'd taken with her. Jesse couldn't find her usual sweatshirt, or her big army surplus backpack. He thought some of the stacks of books and music looked shorter than usual, but he spotted the cassette tape of Crys' latest favourite album sitting on her nightstand in a nest of pencils, rubber bands, crumpled up tissues, paper clips and bits of string. *Under the Pink* by Tori Amos. It had only come out that year, right around the time they left the city. Wouldn't Crys have taken the tape along with her Walkman?

Jesse opened the drawer of the nightstand. Inside was more junk, and a King James Bible.

Crys had hollowed out part of the Bible with an X-Acto knife. She kept her drugs there. Weed, acid, stolen Valium, sometimes even packs of cigarettes. She refused to let Jesse try drugs, but she trusted him enough to let him know where she hid her stash.

Admiring the craftsmanship of the hollow Bible — you'd never know it wasn't a regular book from looking at the outside — Jesse opened it to the deep, perfectly square secret compartment. He expected to find nothing.

There was a full baggie of weed inside, some rolling papers and an orange plastic lighter. Jesse's insides lurched. Maybe Crys hadn't run away after all! But if she hadn't, then where was she? What if something worse had happened to her?

No, said a quiet, cold, grown-up sounding part of Jesse's mind. *She ran, all right. She did exactly what she said she was going to do. Why would she take her weed with her when she'll be back with Marcus soon and able to smoke all she wants for free, because he likes her so much? As for the tape, her tastes change all the time. Last year she loved David Bowie, and now she barely listens to him. She used to like Mom's old hippie music and now she says she can't stand any of it.*

Jesse decided to take the Bible back to his room. He told himself he was just hanging on to it. Once their parents realised Crys was gone, they'd search through all her things. The *police* would search through all her things. Jesse didn't want his sister getting into even more trouble, if they ever caught her.

He didn't know if he wanted them to catch her or not.

Jesse's stomach growled, so he went downstairs to make grilled cheese sandwiches, like he'd planned to in the first place. One for him, one for Mom. Routines and rituals settled his mind, made it easier to get a handle on things. Making sandwiches was useful: predictable and the same procedure every time. He could think while he was cooking.

(Slice a tomato. Get out four pieces of bread and four pre-packaged cheese slices.)

Should he tell Mom that Crys was gone? He probably ought to, right? She'd find out soon enough, anyway.

(Butter both sides of the bread. Grease the skillet.)

She'd find out soon enough, anyway. Didn't he owe it to Crys not to rat her out? To give her as much of a head start as possible? What if she was right about their parents wanting to lock her up in an institution or send her to some kind of boot camp? No, Mom and Dad wouldn't do that.

(Put the sandwiches together. Bread, cheese, tomato slice, cheese, bread.)

Mom wouldn't do that. Dad wouldn't do that.

They were kind, gentle people. They always said they loved Crys and Jesse. Mom cried when Crys acted out, said Crys was breaking her heart. She just wanted Crys to be a happy, normal girl. She bought Crys dresses and cute shoes in hopes that she'd wear them, and tried to get her to make friends with people who didn't sell weed. Dad had hit Crys once, but he said he was really sorry afterwards. He wouldn't have done it if she hadn't been screaming in his face.

(The sandwiches go in the skillet. Wait for the sizzle and the smell of toast, then flip. Make sure the cheese gets nice and gooey.)

He would take Mom's sandwich out to the garden shed she'd turned into her studio. He wouldn't say anything about Crys. But if she asked about Crys, he wouldn't lie to her.

Jesse's mom took the plate of grilled cheese with a smile. There was a big grey splotch of clay on her cheek. "Thank you, sweetheart."

"So. Uh. How's it going out here?"

"Not too bad! Would you like to see my newest vases? I'm working on a tea set right now, too."

Jesse wasn't in the mood to look at pottery, but he didn't feel like he could say no. Besides, it wasn't like holing up in his room to worry about Crys would achieve anything.

The inside of the shed was dominated by a

kiln, which made it even hotter than the sticky summer air outside. Jesse wasn't sure how his mother could stand it all day, even with the two standing fans she kept on full blast. The air near the kiln shimmered with heat and he could feel sweat beginning to prickle his skin.

The rest of the space was as cluttered as Crys' room, but it was tidier clutter. It made Jesse more uncomfortable, though; there was something unpleasant about the texture of the clay. When it was damp, it looked slimy. When it was dry, but unglazed and unfired, it looked like compressed ashes. Like if you touched it, it would crumble immediately into a residue that clung to the cracks in your palms and the little hairs inside your nose.

The finished pieces were pretty: smooth, symmetrical, dripping with oil-slick rainbows of glaze. They all had a chunky solidity to them that was normally reassuring to Jesse, satisfying to balance in his hands. Today, he couldn't stop thinking about what would happen if you hit someone over the head with one of the bigger vases or jars. If you hit them, and hit them again and again.

The crack of the skull. Sticky blood and brains matting hair.

Jesse shuddered and put the vase he was holding back on its shelf. All that stuff on TV about the murder must have gotten to him.

"I haven't eaten my sandwich yet," he said. "I'm going back to the house. I'm hungry."

"Of course." His mom sounded puzzled. "I'm sorry if I kept you, sweetie. You know, you can eat out here with me, if you want."

"No, that's okay." Jesse was already walking back across the yard. "I'm fine! Honest!"

It was only as he poured himself a glass of juice back in the kitchen that he realised his mom hadn't mentioned Crys at all. Not even a joke about how he preferred to eat with his sister instead of with his mother, or about how Crys should be the one making sandwiches, being older and a girl. Jesse frowned as he took a sip of the juice. That was weird, wasn't it?

The juice had pulp in it. Damn. He'd grabbed the wrong carton. Jesse spit into the sink, then poured the undrunk juice down the drain.

"How was work, dear? You seem tense."

"I don't even want to discuss it, Maddie. This new client is a real pain. Mmmm, this is nice garlic bread."

"Jesse helped make it. He's turning into a regular little cook."

"Is that right! Good job, son. Girls love a guy with a little bit of a domestic side."

Jesse started. His father was speaking to him. He took a moment to process the words. "I'm not all that interested in girls right now, Dad. I won't even start middle school until August."

Jesse's dad winked. "Oh, you'll be interested soon enough." He used the last of his garlic bread to mop up the last smears of spaghetti sauce left on his plate.

Jesse hadn't eaten much. He twirled his fork around in his spaghetti and looked at Crys' empty seat beside him. No one set her place for dinner. No one asked where she'd gone. His conscience gnawed at him. He took a bite of spaghetti. It tasted like glue.

Chew. Chew. Swallow. Deep breath.

"Hey, Mom? Dad?"

Jesse's parents both stopped eating and stared at him. His voice had come out even higher pitched than it usually was, strangled and nervous.

"Is there something wrong, Jesse?" his mother asked.

"Haven't you wondered where Crys is? I mean, all day. She's been missing. Didn't you notice?"

Jesse's parents looked at each other.

"I don't recall seeing her this morning, but I assumed she was asleep. When I came home for dinner, I thought she must be at a friend's house." As though Crys had any friends in Narrowbrook. "Maddie? You must have seen her at some point during the day, right? Did she go to visit someone?"

"Mom hasn't seen her either!" Jesse cut in.

"Don't interrupt, Jesse. No, I'm afraid I haven't seen her either." Jesse's mom wrinkled up her forehead. "That's worrying. Dave, should we call the neighbours? The police?"

"Not yet. She's never run away before, but it wouldn't exactly be a surprise, would it? Maybe she's trying to get back to the city. God knows she won't stop talking about how much she hates it here." Jesse's dad reached for another piece of garlic bread. "I think she'll turn up tomorrow. We wouldn't want to waste police time. Especially not so soon after the shoplifting incident."

"But the neighbours, surely," Jesse's mom insisted.

"Of course! We'll ask around right after we finish eating."

Jesse looked from his mom to his dad and back again. They seemed to have stopped talking to him, or towards him. They were talking to each other instead, and not just with their words. Their eyes were dark and locked together. Their faces seemed strange. There was some other conversation happening between them underneath or behind or beyond the things they said with their mouths, some private, adult conversation. Jesse was so shut out from that conversation he couldn't even guess its content, its general shape. He could only see it was there, hovering silent and ominous.

He forced himself to take another bite of spaghetti. He tried to be happy for Crys. If their parents dawdled on calling the cops, it would give her even more time to get wherever she wanted to go. Back to Marcus and her old haunts, or somewhere entirely new.

The spaghetti slid down Jesse's throat in a gelid lump. The corners of his eyes itched. He asked to be excused from the table.

*

Jesse dreamed he was walking in the woods. They were huge and dark, the trees stark paper-cut-out shadows even when he got close to them. There was no bark. There were no leaves. No texture, no colour, no detail. It was like looking inside a deep hole. He could put his arm through a tree and it would reach into silhouette blackness without end. Branches were rips in the stuff that made the world.

He wasn't scared. The warm air caressed his body — he was naked, for some reason, running naked through the woods even though there might be ticks. Ticks carrying Lyme disease. He didn't care. He didn't even care if he died, and that seemed more and more likely as the void rips in the shape of trees crowded closer and closer, close enough for low branches to graze his shoulders and neck. They left little flares of blood where they touched him, and he still didn't care. He felt excited. Something was coming. He was on the verge of making the most important discovery of his whole life.

The air put its invisible hands on his sweat-slicked hips. It whispered wind words in his ear. Jesse knew he only had to walk a little bit farther, maybe only a few more steps, and he would see—

He woke suddenly, panting, reflexively moving his hands over his crotch. There was sticky, earthy-smelling white stuff all over his bedsheets. It took him an embarrassingly long time to realise he'd had a wet dream. He wasn't sure why. It had been about the woods, about walking through trees that were jagged and black and sharp against his skin. There was nothing sexy about that. He should have been scared in the dream.

Well, he was scared now. Not just of the dream, but of his body's betrayal. He felt like he'd felt when he wet the bed as a five-year-old.

If Crys had been home, he would have gone to her. She would have known what to do about the sheets. Even though she was a girl, she would have reassured him that this was normal and that he'd regain control over his bodily functions in time. She would have said it with such confidence Jesse would never have thought to question her.

But Crys was gone and Jesse had to strip the sheets from his bed and sneak them down to the laundry room alone.

3

"Hey! Hey, Jesse!"

The kid hanging halfway over the low fence between Jesse's yard and the neighbours' was quite familiar, although he and Jesse had never really spoken before. Curly haired, freckled, gap-toothed. Skinny, in loud checkerboard shorts that ballooned out over his giraffe-like knees. What was his name? Stephen? Jesse should know. The boy was in his grade at school, as well as living right next door to him.

"I'm Lane, remember? Lane Thompson? I was in Mrs. McCarty's class last year. I helped your parents with some boxes when you guys first moved in."

Lane, not Stephen. Stephen had been Lane's friend: a stocky kid with thick glasses and a ponytail that made people think he was a girl sometimes. The two boys had been inseparable at the start of the spring semester, but sometime around March they must've fought. Jesse stopped seeing them together at school. Stephen cut his hair and got rid of the glasses. He started hanging out with the guys who were into sports, while Lane… Lane had mostly been alone. Like Jesse.

Jesse assumed Lane didn't try to befriend him back then because he didn't want to get bullied. Now he was bouncing on the balls of his feet with excitement. He kept waving his arms to get Jesse's attention.

Jesse came over to the fence. "Lane. Yeah, I remember you. You've never said hi to me before."

"Sorry." Lane wrinkled his nose. "I felt… I dunno, intimidated."

"Worried you'd catch something from Greer the Queer?"

"Dude! No! People said that stuff about me and Stephen, too. It's all retarded."

"That's another thing they call me, yeah."

"Sorry. I mean, you just seemed so cool and different. You were always reading weird books and making those little statues out of the aluminium foil your mom wrapped your lunches in."

"I wrap my own lunches, mostly. What'd you wanna talk to me about, anyway?"

"Is it true your sister's missing? Crystal?" Lane was practically levitating. "I overheard my mom talking about it on the phone. She ran away, right? Was it a drug thing? One time Casey Aster told me your sister dropped acid. At *school*. His big brother told him."

"What does Casey Aster know about anything?" said Jesse, who had no idea if Crys ever dropped acid at school. It did sound like the kind of thing she might do.

"Casey Aster knows *everything* that goes on at the high school," Lane replied sagely. "Anyway, I think it's cool. I think Crystal is cool. She's different, too."

"Thanks." Jesse's throat felt clogged and sore all of a sudden. His eyes tingled. *Don't cry*. He didn't, but his voice sounded full of tears anyway. "She did run away. Mom and Dad are waiting until tomorrow to call the cops. If she's not back by tonight, I mean."

"Aw, hey." Incredibly, Lane reached across the fence to pat Jesse's head, like he was a dog or a cat. Even more incredibly, it felt sort of nice. "I'm sure she's gonna be fine. They'll find her."

"That's not—" Jesse stopped himself. He wasn't sure if he wanted Crys to be found or not. He wasn't sure which of these outcomes would be good for her, which one would make her happy and safe. If anything could make her happy and safe. "Her name's Crys," he said, instead. "She doesn't like when people she likes call her Crystal."

"You think she'd like me?" Lane grinned. "Dude, is it true she smokes weed?"

Small town kids. Jesse snorted. "Of course she smokes weed. She does acid and shrooms and bennies. Weed is almost not even a real drug compared to those." He kept looking over Lane's bouncing shoulder and into his yard. It wasn't nearly as big as Jesse's yard, but it was much tidier. Jesse liked the evenness of the cut grass, and how bright its green looked in the afternoon sunshine. He wished he could mow a lawn that perfect.

"Bennies?" Lane asked.

"Like Valium and Xanax."

"Okay." Lane clearly didn't know, or care, what those were. "So if it's almost not even a real drug, do you think she'd let me try some? When she gets back. I could pay her ten dollars!"

Jesse looked closely at Lane's face. He was lopsided and messy, with his splatter of freckles across the nose and hair flying every which way. His eyebrows were barely there, giving him a perpetual expression of surprise, but his eyelashes were thick and black and super long. Jesse didn't want to like him. Lane was nauseatingly peppy, a dumb kid without a care in the world. He'd be handsome and charming and popular with girls in a few years.

Despite his inner protestations, Jesse could feel liking take root in his chest all the same. Jesse didn't want Lane to go away. He wanted to impress him so much that Lane would *have* to keep talking to him when school started back up.

"Keep your ten dollars," said Jesse. "I can get you some weed."

Lane's eyes widened. "Really?!"

"Yeah. I just need a few minutes."

"Okay, okay, great! Hey, you wanna smoke it together? You can show me how! We'll go to my treehouse and hang out."

"Sure thing." Jesse was relieved that his voice came out sounding cool and calm this time. His heart was beating like a hummingbird's wings.

Lane's treehouse was in the woods that began — or ended — right behind the Thompsons' and the Greers' property. Jesse knew that the woods weren't that big by adult-world standards, but they seemed pretty big to him. He felt like he and Lane had walked at least a mile by the time they reached the oak where the treehouse perched. The tree had boards nailed into its trunk to serve as a ladder. A thick rope hung down from an upper bough; a few feet below where the rope was tied, a large platform with short plywood walls on three sides was wedged between the oak's sturdy branches. The side facing the tree trunk was open.

"I thought you said this was a tree *house,*" said Jesse, craning his neck to see the whole structure. Sweat ran down his back and into the waistband of his underwear.

"Maybe it's not fancy, but it's a fantastic place. You'll see! You'll love it." Lane started climbing up the board ladder. Some of the boards made creaking sounds.

Jesse tucked the hollow Bible into his armpit,

took a deep breath and followed Lane. He was clumsy, since he could use only one arm freely, but he managed.

The treehouse, or tree platform, seemed smaller and higher up once they were in it. Jesse and Lane were forced to stand up, or sit very close together.

When Jesse stood, the plywood walls came to his waist and the ground looked dizzyingly far off. He could see the roof of his house and the roof of Lane's through a tangle of branches, peeking out over the tops of some smaller evergreens and maples. When he sat down, his knee knocking against Lane's by accident, the walls rose up over his head and he felt cut off from everything but the sky and the oak spreading out above him. Protected. Adrift on a sea of leaves.

"This is pretty neat," he admitted. His hands fluttered at his sides.

"Told you! You brought the stuff, right?"

Jesse showed Lane the hollow Bible; Lane was appropriately awed. It took a few tries, but Jesse managed to roll a joint the way he'd seen Crys do. Lane wanted to light it and take the first toke, so Jesse let him.

Lane inhaled deeply and the end of the joint glowed like a devil's eye. Then he started coughing and hacking. He thrust the joint at Jesse and doubled over, pressing his hands to his chest and stomach.

Jesse took note. He inhaled very shallowly. When his throat started to burn and itch, he only pretended to take a second puff before passing the joint back to Lane.

Lane's eyes were red and watery. "Man. It must be, like, really strong, right? But look at you. So cool. I can tell you've done this before."

Jesse tried to look mature: a man of the world. "You'll get used to it. Lots of people cough their first time."

"Yeah." Lane inhaled again and made a face.

They were quiet for a while, watching clouds pass overhead. Light shimmered through the forest greenery. A white butterfly or moth spiralled into the treehouse, rested a moment on the floor beside Jesse's sneakers and took off again. The boys passed the joint back and forth. Lane's eyes got redder and redder and his pupils got bigger and bigger. Jesse wasn't inhaling, so he didn't think he should be getting high, but everything around him seemed magnified and dreamlike. Lane's mouth was slightly open and Jesse noticed the little bumps on the lower edges of his front teeth, the beautiful gloss of spit on his teeth and lips.

"What're you looking at?" Lane's voice was slow. It wobbled.

"Nothing. Just looking."

"Are you thinking about your sister?"

Jesse looked up. Had he ever noticed how *blue* the sky was before? "Yeah. I guess."

"Tell me about her?"

Jesse didn't want to talk about Crys with some boy he barely knew. But something about the way Lane said it, like he was asking a casual question, and something about Lane himself and something about the bright dome of the sky, like a cartoon sky with its cotton candy clouds, made Jesse's mouth start moving.

He told Lane how Crys had always been different from most people. More fearless and adventurous. Constantly moving, quick to anger but also quick to delight. She hated rules and she hated to do the things people expected of her. Their parents had called her a tomboy. Dad said she was sensitive. Mom said she had emotional problems. They both said she'd outgrow it.

Instead, when Crys became a teenager, she started skipping school and doing drugs. She shoplifted. She hung out with guys who were three or four or eight years older than she was. She cut her wrists until her arms looked like birch trees. She began having what their parents called 'moods' and then 'depressions'. Crys called these her 'blue periods'. During a blue period, she would shut herself up in her room for days and days, not even letting Jesse in to see her. Not showering. Not eating much of anything. Not listening to music.

Their parents tried talking to Crys. They tried punishing her. They made her see a shrink for a while and take the pills Crys said made her feel shaky and nauseous. When Crys got suspended from her nice private school for the fourth time, they tried sending her to an 'alternative education program'. ("That means it's for druggies, delinquents and dropouts," Crys had explained to Jesse.)

The alternative education program was good because it was where Crys met Marcus and a few other weird people she seemed to get along with. Crys got a lot happier there. She didn't have blue periods. She actually went to school more often than not. But she was still doing drugs and shoplifting and having sex with her older boyfriends. Since the alternative education program didn't have uniforms, she could wear her baggy black sweatshirt and boys' jeans every single day. She came home in a cop car a couple of times.

Then they moved to Narrowbrook. Jesse's parents never said that they'd moved because of Crys. But his mom kept talking about Narrowbrook's superior public schools, how it wasn't good for kids to grow up in an 'urban environment' and how much good the trees and lawns and fresh air and quiet would do Crys. Jesse, too. That wasn't how things turned out, of course. At least, not for Crys.

Jesse stopped talking when he started to feel tears building behind his eyes. He wasn't going to cry and he definitely wasn't going to cry in front of Lane.

"Whoa," said Lane. "She sounds badass. I hope I get to meet her someday. I'm sorry your parents didn't understand her." He grabbed the toe of Jesse's shoe and wiggled it back and forth like it was a loose tooth.

Jesse smiled. He imagined he could feel Lane's fingertips through the shoe rubber. It was weird, but sort of nice. "What the hell, Lane. Do you have a crush on my sister or something?"

Lane snorted. "No!"

"Your loss." Jesse put his hand over Lane's on the shoe and wiggled it back and forth with him. Then he shut his eyes and said, without wanting to or knowing he was about to say it, "I'm really, really afraid that a bad thing might've happened to her. I'm afraid she could be dead."

As he spoke the words he realised they were true. The summer world was beautiful, but it smelled like rotting weeds. He kept thinking about things decaying. He kept feeling sick, sick the same way Crys had felt sick on those psych meds.

"How come?"

"I don't know, exactly. It's this feeling I have that won't go away."

Lane grabbed Jesse's hand and pulled him forward into an awkward hug. Jesse's nose got smushed into Lane's sweaty collarbone. The other boy still smelled like a kid, salty and clean and alive under all the pot smoke. Jesse let himself relax, although part of him wanted to tear himself away. He could feel Lane's heart-beat.

"Crys is super tough and she's gonna be fine," said Lane. "She's probably having all kinds of adventures right now. You gotta stay chill. Stay strong. It's okay."

"You don't know that. You *can't* know that."

"I know," said Lane."I know, I know, I know." He rubbed Jesse's back.

Jesse tried to look up at Lane's face. Was this a weird thing for boys to do? He thought it might be. Lane's eyes were half-lidded and black. Jesse's stomach lurched like he was at the top of a rollercoaster. He felt his penis start to press painfully against the zipper of his jeans.

It was too much, suddenly. Everything was too much. The plywood walls of the treehouse seemed to shake and shimmer. Jesse could see each one of Lane's long eyelashes casting a separate shadow on his smooth, freckled cheeks. He moved back, closing in on himself. He wanted to go home. He felt kind of like he needed to pee. He was scared.

"I really like you," said Lane. "We should be friends."

"I want to go home," said Jesse. He was already standing, lurching like he was on the deck of a ship at sea, groping for the ladder.

"Wait," said Lane.

Jesse had reached the rope. He didn't trust himself not to fall from the boards of the ladder. The rope would be much faster, anyway. He grabbed it and slid down. His hands felt scoured, stung, burned.

"Jesse!" Lane called. "Wait! I didn't mean—"

Jesse hit the ground in a stumbling run. Insects screamed all around him. He didn't want to be anywhere near Lane. He didn't want to be anywhere near anybody.

He pressed his hands over his ears and ran away from the treehouse, away from his house and Lane's house, farther into the woods.

When Jesse's aching sides and burning lungs forced him to stop running, he found himself much deeper into the woods than he'd known it was possible to go.

The trees loomed and blocked out most of the sky. Light fell in dusty shafts through cracks in the canopy of branches and leaves. Jesse had a good sense of direction, but now he felt lost and disoriented. He knew which direction he'd come from — he thought — and he was sure he should be close to the highway now. The woods, he reminded himself again, weren't that big. They were cordoned off by housing developments on two sides and the highway on a third. In the fourth direction, they dwindled into a meadow, a bike trail and a dirt road before meeting the river.

Jesse listened. He could hear no rush of traffic. He must have gotten turned around. But he couldn't hear the river, either, or any sound of people out enjoying the summer afternoon. No lawnmowers, no kids shouting, no barking dogs, no radio shows or music crackling from outdoor speakers. Jesse shivered, although his shirt was sticking to him and his hair was damp with sweat. He couldn't even hear birds or insects anymore. The only sounds in this forest were the rustle of leaves and his own laboured breathing. It reminded him of the dream he had the night before, although it was broad daylight. His hard-on was gone, but he still felt an uncomfortable, tingling pressure in his groin.

Jesse forced himself to walk forward. If he just kept going in a straight line, he'd reach the highway soon, or the river, or the back of somebody's house, and then he could figure out where he was.

He thought the trees looked like they thinned out to the left of him, so that was the direction he chose. He wished he'd brought his compass. Crys had made fun of him for having it because it was nerdy and because they'd lived in the city and had never gone camping or anything. But Jesse knew it might come in handy one day. Too bad he'd left it at home.

The dirt under Jesse's feet looked darker than regular dirt and there were little sparkles in it.

Like stars in the blackness of space. Jesse thought the sparkles might be mica. Or maybe they were organic, some kind of bug egg. Or bug poop.

Huge, buckled roots disrupted the ground and the sparkly dirt, even as the space between the trees grew wider and wider. Jesse had to watch his feet to see that he didn't trip over any. The trees all seemed to be oaks now, tall and wide and probably older than the Declaration of Independence.

Everything remained eerily silent. There were deep green diamonds and squares of light all over the forest floor from sunshine falling through the leaves. Their patterns shifted like a kaleidoscope. Sometimes, for a brief moment, they seemed to shimmer strange new colours like violet, hot pink and indigo as they picked up the glitter from the black ground.

Suddenly, Jesse emerged from the cover of the oaks. There was no road and no river and no house in sight. He was standing at the edge of a small, circular clearing, surrounded by massive oak trees on every side. Long grass and wild-flowers came up to his knees. Huge mushrooms sprouted everywhere. Some of them looked like bloated human fingers. Some of them looked like greasy puddings.

Jesse shivered again. Mushrooms creeped him out a little. The way they were more biologically similar to animals than to plants. He didn't even like to eat them on pizza.

He took a deep breath and stepped into the clearing, careful to avoid the fungi. At least he was in full sunshine again, under a blue sky. Maybe it was lucky he'd gotten a little lost. It gave him time to calm down from whatever happened up in the treehouse. Maybe he *had* gotten stoned. His head felt a lot clearer now.

He had to be getting close to the edge of the woods. He *had* to be.

The clearing smelled bad, not like grass and wildflowers, not even like rotting plants. It was a dead animal smell. Jesse kept an eye out to make sure he didn't step in a raccoon or possum. His sneakers were almost-new and now they were hopelessly scuffed and smeared with forest debris. All he needed was to get guts and brains and stuff on them. Mom wasn't going to be happy.

The bad smell got stronger as Jesse approached the centre of the clearing. He could even see the animal's body now, close ahead of him, long and dark where it made an indentation in the grass. It was way too big to be a raccoon. Maybe a dog? A small deer? No, that was fabric, not fur or hide. Clothes.

Jesse's heart raced. He gagged. It was a dead *person*.

He didn't want to look, but he felt an obligation. He had a suspicion. He hoped he was wrong.

The body was sprawled on its side among tall stalks of light-blue bell-shaped flowers and grass that looked like wheat. Its mud-splattered black sweatshirt was torn. Its hands were bloated and yellowish. Its hair was so matted with blood it was hard to tell what colour it had been. The back of its head was a mess of thick, scabby dried blood, sharp skull fragments and churned brains baking slowly in the heat.

A bloodstained rock sat near the body. It was smooth, like it had been polished or worn down through years of handling. There was a symbol painted or drawn on it in black ink. Jesse tried to follow the lines of the symbol, but they made him dizzy and were partly obscured by the blood and the position of the rock.

He had read about ritual murders and human sacrifices. He knew what kind of thing he was looking at. Part of him wasn't even that surprised. With all the newspaper articles and daytime TV shows warning of Satanic cults and Satanic child abuse and Satanic murder, it seemed like something he should prepare himself to encounter as he grew older.

If Crys had met a Satanist, she would probably have gone off with him in a heartbeat. She would probably think he was the coolest guy she'd ever met.

Jesse walked slowly around the body. He wanted to see its face. There were no buzzing flies or wriggling maggots in the bowl of its broken head, no insects busy with the work of taking apart the dead. That seemed worse to him, somehow, than if there had been. Everything was quiet and still and reeking.

Jesse knelt so the grass and flowers stretched over his head. He and the corpse were alone now, in a sealed off room apart from the rest of nature.

Jesse looked into the corpse's half-lidded, rolled back eyes. Its mouth gaped open wider than Jesse ever imagined mouths could go. The face was distorted, but there was no question that it belonged to Crys.

Jesse didn't realise he was screaming until he'd run across to the other side of the field and far into the trees.

4

His voice gave out eventually, but he kept trying to scream anyway. Thorns tore at his clothes and skin. Birdsong and the incessant buzzing of insects came back. Dogs began to bark somewhere close by. He ran towards the sound, making a weak, hoarse wailing noise.

Jesse burst into a stranger's backyard, having reached the end of the woods as he knew he would. Only he must've gotten turned around somehow; after a moment of disorientation, he recognised the grey-blue siding and shingled roof of the house in front of him, and he knew it was a house at the other end of his street. He didn't know whom it belonged to. Probably the blonde woman who looked up from pruning a rosebush in astonishment as Jesse struggled over a short chain-link fence and fell to his scraped knees in the grass, panting and sweaty and begging for help in disjointed sentence fragments.

The blonde woman took Jesse inside the kitchen of the grey-blue house, making soothing noises and promising to get his parents right away. Jesse gave her their home phone number and their address, then sat shaking at the table, too tense to drink the glass of ice water the woman had set in front of him. He wanted to tell her she needed to call the cops, too, but he couldn't find it in him to speak. Not yet.

The blonde woman went into the hall, where there was an old-fashioned rotary phone. Jesse heard her dialling. He heard her chirpy "Hello? Am I speaking with Mrs. Greer?"

A boy Jesse's age entered the kitchen through a door by the stove. It took Jesse a moment to recognise Stephen outside the context of school. His hair had grown out a little, but it was still very short. He wore a button-up collared shirt and his large grey eyes had an empty look that made Jesse remember Crys' dead face and flinch away.

Stephen blinked. He walked to the fridge and poured himself a glass of milk and sat down across from Jesse.

"Hey," he said. "Are you all right?" He rubbed at his left eye. Trouble with his contacts, Jesse realised.

Stephen waited a moment for a response. When he didn't get one, he started drinking his milk in polite little sips, like an adult would drink coffee.

The blonde woman came back. "Your mom and dad will be right over," she assured Jesse. "You worried them, you know. They didn't know where you were for hours. But they said to tell you they've got good news—" she switched track as she noticed Stephen's presence, "—oh! And I see you've met my stepson! Stephen, I hope you haven't been bothering Jesse here."

Jesse shook his head. "No," he whispered. "He hasn't."

"It was nice to meet you," said Stephen absently. He finished his milk. He carried the empty glass to the dishwasher, then drifted out of the room. Jesse was relieved to see him go.

"Anyway!" the blonde woman chirped. "The good news! Jesse, your older sister Crystal returned home this afternoon. She got back about thirty, forty minutes ago, so she might be tired, but your mother said she'd try and convince her to come pick you up along with your parents. They all know how upset you've been since she ran off the other day."

It took a while for Jesse to process these words.

"Crys came back? She's alive?"

"Of course she's alive. It doesn't sound like she got far. Narrowbrook is a very safe town."

Jesse *knew* he hadn't imagined the body in the woods. He knew whose it was. There was no way he would mistake some stranger for Crys. Was there?

"No way," he muttered to himself, hoping the blonde woman wouldn't hear.

Although Jesse was less than a block from their house, his parents drove over in the minivan. Crys came with them — it was undeniably Crys. Her shaggy hair and black sweatshirt and boys' jeans were the same as ever. She looked tired and vacant, her face oddly smoothed out, somehow younger and older at the same time. When she stepped out of the van's side door, Jesse ran to her at once, shouting her name.

She stood in the driveway like a post and allowed him to hug her. After a moment, her arms came up around him and she gave his back a few soft, tentative pats.

Jesse's parents made polite small talk with the blonde woman, who was called Helen or Mrs. Morrow. Then they hugged Jesse and told him not to go anywhere without telling them ever again. "That goes for both of you," Dad said, pointing at Jesse and Crys in turn. "I don't need any more disappearing children this summer."

"What had you so scared?" Mom asked as they buckled themselves into their seats. "Mrs. Morrow says you seemed almost hysterical."

Jesse only hesitated for a moment. There was still a dead body in the woods, even if it wasn't Crys, and adults ought to know about it. They'd handle the situation, somehow. Carefully, he told his mother most of the story: leaving out the weed, the strange energy he'd felt between himself and Lane and the part where he'd thought the corpse belonged to Crys. By the time he finished, they'd driven home and moved into the living room. In fact, by the time he finished, they had all been in the living room for quite some time. It was a very short drive, and the story was not an easy story to tell. His parents sat with Crys on the sofa while he paced across the floor.

"— and, I don't know, it scared me real bad. I'd never seen a dead person in real life before, let alone one who got murdered. And she was just a kid, really. Maybe sixteen, seventeen. Or younger."

Jesse fell silent. His family stared at him.

"A Satanic ritual, huh?" said Dad, raising his eyebrows. "Jesse, are you sure about that?"

"David," Mom admonished. She looked at Jesse with moist, concerned eyes. "I'll contact the police. If there's a dead body in those woods, they'll find it. Jesse, you did the right thing trusting us with this and you don't need to worry about it any more."

Crys tipped her head to one side. "You should stay out of the woods," she said, without emotion.

"Yes," Mom said, with force. "I don't want you playing in those woods. I'm going to tell Mrs. Thompson that Lane shouldn't be playing there, either. I doubt there are Satanists lurking in the bushes, but it isn't safe."

"I saw a symbol on the rock," Jesse insisted. He felt stupid and childish, but he knew what he'd seen. He wasn't the type of boy who imagined things.

"You were very scared," said his mother. "You were probably in shock."

"You got confused," said his father. "Your mind might've made up all kinds of details. Son, things like that just don't happen in real life, no matter what those nuts on daytime television tell you. There's no devil."

"It's nothing to be ashamed of. You were very brave in how you handled the situation," his mother insisted in a consoling tone.

Jesse didn't feel brave at all. He felt sick. The living room smelled cloyingly of fake fruit cleaning liquid. There was a crack in the plaster of the wall behind the sofa. Crys' unfocused eyes reminded him of Stephen's, which reminded him of the body in the woods. (Not Crys' body. *Not* hers.) Jesse's stomach growled, but the thought of eating made him want to vomit.

He ran upstairs to his bedroom. Mom was calling out to him, but he ignored her. He lay face down on his little kid sheets printed with rocket ships and ringed planets, faded but clean. He didn't bother taking off his clothes and he didn't come out when his parents knocked, asking him if he was all right, telling him dinner was ready.

He thought he might respond if Crys came to talk to him, if she told him where she'd been and what had happened to her.

But she never knocked on the door, or opened it without knocking, or called his name.

*

Jesse dreamed he was walking through the woods again. This time, they were bright and detailed. This time, the branches of the trees slipped harmlessly off his skin and clothes where they touched him. This time, he was afraid. He didn't know what he was scared of, but he knew it was coming to get him and he knew he couldn't do anything about it. It would get him whether he ran or stayed still, whether he tried to hide or tried to fight. He kept walking because it didn't make a difference and his heart thudded against his ribs.

There were no sounds in the forest. A white butterfly or moth fluttered ahead of him for a while. It seemed like it was trying to lead him, but Jesse wasn't sure if he could trust it. He kept walking in a straight line and eventually the winged creature gave up.

Jesse walked through his dreams for what felt like years. The trees never ended. There was always something coming to get him. But it never arrived and he never found out what it was.

He woke sweating and short of breath. He didn't open his eyes for several minutes in case it would turn out he was still in the forest.

5

In the morning, Jesse felt much better, at least physically.

He was ravenous, maybe from all the walking he'd done in his nightmare. Fortunately, Dad made pancakes. Light and fluffy with blueberries and bananas, the way Jesse and Crys both liked them. Crys was awake in time for breakfast, for once, and she and Jesse ate together at the table. Jesse had wolfed down several pancakes drenched in syrup before he noticed that Crys was only picking at hers, taking delicate, fussy bites. That was unlike her. She didn't put butter or syrup on the pancakes, either, and instead of orange juice or coffee she was drinking a glass of milk. Crys hated to drink straight milk, claiming it felt like drinking a glass of watery pus.

Jesse thought about saying something. He decided not to. Crys didn't need to be needled right now.

"Well, I'm glad to see you've both got your appetites back," Dad said jovially, although Crys hadn't. "Jesse, the police are searching those woods right now. They'll let us know as soon as they find anything."

Jesse nodded. Crys asked to be excused from the table. Her voice was quiet, without a trace of sarcasm or impatience.

"Why don't you just leave if you're done?" asked Jesse, frowning.

"Jesse!" Dad said. "Don't be rude to your sister."

"I was asking a question!"

"Crystal, that's very polite of you, but there's no need to ask permission. Put your plate in the dishwasher, okay?" Dad poured a packet of artificial sweetener into his coffee and took a long, steaming gulp.

As Crys scraped her barely eaten pancakes into the garbage can, the doorbell chimed. Then it chimed again. Jesse went to answer it. He was full, and he thought it might be Lane. He wasn't sure if he wanted to see Lane again right now, but, for reasons he couldn't articulate to himself, the idea of his mom or dad interacting with Lane, even briefly, was unbearable.

The man on the doorstep was not Lane, although he was also curly-haired and gangling. He was parent-age, in his forties maybe, and he wore a polo shirt tucked into jeans that looked like they'd been ironed. He smiled down at Jesse in a bland, absentminded sort of way.

His eyes were grey and shallow-looking. Jesse immediately thought of Stephen's eyes, of the not-Crys corpse's eyes, of Crys' eyes since her return. He hoped this wasn't permanent, that he wasn't going to be catapulted into a chain of eyeball-related memories leading back to the clearing in the woods every time he saw a person with grey eyes, forever.

"Hi," said the man on the doorstep. "You must be Jesse."

"Yeah?"

"I'm your friend Lane's father. He said you left this behind when you came to play with him the other day." The man removed Crys' Bible from where he'd had it tucked under the crook of his right arm and offered it to Jesse, who snatched it away at once.

"It's nice to see a boy your age taking interest in matters of faith."

Jesse glared. Was Lane's dad making fun of him? Had he seen what was inside Crys' Bible?

"Lane would have brought it over himself, but he said you two had an argument and you might not want to talk to him right now. He told me to tell you he's sorry for any misunderstanding." Mr. Thompson's teeth were very flat and very white. He seemed sincere.

"Thanks," said Jesse awkwardly. "Tell him thanks for me."

"Of course." Mr. Thompson turned on his heel and walked away without another word. His movements were somehow both graceful and stiff.

"Who was at the door?" called Jesse's dad from the kitchen, not sounding particularly interested.

"Nobody," Jesse called back. "Some guy who wanted to give me a Bible."

Jesse sat on Crys' bed with the Bible in his lap, waiting. He had expected her to come upstairs immediately after she finished her breakfast, but she must have found something to do elsewhere in the house. Jesse couldn't imagine what.

Someone had changed Crys' sheets and made her bed. The sheets and blanket and quilt were folded under the mattress in neat hospital corners. They lay so flat and tight that Jesse thought it'd be almost impossible to get under them. There were no crumbs in sight.

Jesse was just about to put a record on, even though the only ones of Crys' he really liked were They Might Be Giants and *Tea for the Tillerman*, which she didn't listen to anymore, when Crys finally appeared in the doorway.

"Jesse," she said, sounding unsurprised. "You're in my bedroom."

"What happened to your *face*?" Crys looked wrong: flushed, bloody-mouthed, but above all different in some unsettling and all-encompassing way he couldn't pin down.

Then he looked at her more closely and it clicked: she was wearing makeup. Mascara, eyeliner, lipstick, blush. He had never seen Crys in makeup before.

"Do you like it? Mom helped me put it on. I was tired of looking washed out." Crys knelt beside Jesse and began thumbing through her record collection.

"It's... it's different." Jesse stared at Crys, trying to read her expression. He couldn't. Her hair was different, too. It was pinned back so it no longer fell over her eyes like a curtain when she leaned forward. Little jewelled clips cradled her forehead like a crown. "What do you want to listen to?"

Crys examined the cover of *Germfree Adolescents,* where young punks posed inside giant test tubes. She squinted at their mugging expressions and cheap, bright clothes. "Ugh. Not this." Back in the milk crate of records it went. Crys flipped through several more, dismissing each with the same level of mild disgust. "You know, I don't think I need to keep *any* of these."

"What do you mean, 'keep'?"

"Take a look around this room, Jesse. It's all cluttered up." She sounded like Mom. "I'm going to clean it out. Get rid of all the old stuff. Books and records first. I guess the clothes will have to stay for now. Until I can get some nice dresses and blouses. Jeans that actually fit."

"Why would you want dresses and blouses?"

"Why wouldn't I? It's time for a change, Jess."

Jesse's sense that something terrible had happened to Crys during her absence grew. She didn't seem sad, or traumatised, exactly, but this abrupt need to get rid of everything she loved was almost worse. If Crys had been upset, Jesse would have known how to talk to her, how to comfort her. This new Crys was an inscrutable stranger, and he felt as shy and tongue-tied in her presence as he would in the presence of any teenager he didn't know. She might do or say anything at all. Her feelings were locked up behind opaque niceties and mysterious body language.

"But what are you going to do with the books and records?" Jesse's voice came out tremulous and whiny.

"Put them out by the curb on bulk trash day, I guess." Crys shrugged. "Maybe I'll give them to the thrift store."

"You can't! What if you change your mind and you want them back?"

"If you're so concerned about them, you can take them," said Crys, sounding bored.

"I will!" Jesse spoke before he thought. Immediately after the words left his mouth, he realised how much space Crys' stuff would take up in his room. He remembered that he didn't even like most of her music, and he wasn't sure he wanted to read any of her books. But if the alternative was that Crys would throw it all away, or give it all away to strangers…

"Just make sure you keep them tidy," Crys told him. "I won't be responsible for any more messes."

"Okay." Jesse remembered why he'd come to see Crys in the first place. "Crys, I'm really sorry but… I took your Bible while you were gone. I thought you didn't want it anymore. I shared some of the stuff with my friend Lane, and today he brought the Bible back. Well, his dad did. But I don't think he looked inside!"

Crys blinked. "Bible?" she asked. "Why would I have a Bible?"

"You know. Your special Bible. The one you fixed up so it would hold… things."

"What kinds of things?"

"You know." Jesse cupped his hand beside his mouth and whispered. "*Drugs*."

God, he sounded dorky. He waited for Crys to laugh, or at least roll her eyes.

Instead, the faint look of disgust returned. "Oh," she said flatly. "No, I don't want those back. You shouldn't keep them, either. Please throw it all away."

"Throw it away?!"

"Yes. Take it out of this room immediately. Get rid of it." She gave Jesse a push to get him started. Her hands were very strong and very cold.

*

The glowing red lines of his digital clock said 3:58 a.m. Jesse had never been awake so late before. Or maybe it was early. His ceiling fan groaned and whirred. A white moth flitted through his open window and hovered above one of the cardboard box's peeled-back flaps. Jesse moved carefully so as not to disturb it.

He was going through all the belongings he'd moved out of Crys' room and into his own. They'd been living in his closet and under his bed and stacked beside his bed like a table for the past week. A week during which Crys had only become more distant from him. She wouldn't talk about the past, about the city or about their conversation the night she left. She wouldn't talk about what happened to her during the two days she was missing. She didn't even want him to call her Crys anymore. She was Crystal again, now.

Crystal was an even-tempered, soft-spoken girl who wore makeup and blouses with puffy sleeves. She spent a lot of time with Mom. Jesse often heard them laughing quietly together through the walls, when they'd always fought before. Crystal got her earlobes pierced at the mall and wore a pair of rhinestone earrings with gold backs. Crystal kept her room sparkling clean. She cleaned the rest of the house too, while Mom and Dad were working.

Jesse caught her waxing and polishing the

floor one morning. He hadn't known that was something people did in real life, in modern times. He stared at Crystal, kneeling with her sleeves rolled up and her new earrings shining like the honey-coloured wood.

There weren't cuts on her arms anymore. There weren't even any raised scars there. Jesse felt dread start to gnaw at his stomach. That was impossible, wasn't it? Her cuts had never healed so quickly before. And scars were supposed to be permanent. He tried to tell himself it was a trick of the light, or maybe Mom had shown her how to cover them really well with makeup. But the more he stared, the more he was sure: all evidence of his sister's self-inflicted wounds had been erased. Crystal's arms were smooth and blemishless from wrist to elbow.

Crystal glanced up at Jesse. "Why are you staring at me that way?"

"You don't have to do that," said Jesse, who couldn't think of anything else to say. Talking to Crystal seemed more impossible by the day.

"But I want to," said Crystal, returning to her task.

Pod person, Jesse thought as he went back upstairs. *Imposter*. The thought never left him after that, although he knew he was probably being childish. What evidence did he have? Disappearing scars and a dead body he thought he saw when he was high on secondhand pot smoke. His own hurt feelings and growing anxiety.

Still, he missed Crys. He had never missed anyone before. He wasn't sure what to do, what would help, if anything could make it go away, if things would ever return to the way they'd been. He couldn't confide in anyone, of course, or ask for advice. They'd tell him his sister was right there. Crystal was fine and safe, and doing better than ever. What did he have to be upset about?

Jesse stopped sleeping well. His dreams got longer and more vivid, and they were always about walking through endless trees, pursued by something unknown and horrible, or looking for something he never found. Tonight, he wasn't able to fall asleep at all.

After hours of lying on his back in bed listening to the fan and staring into the grainy night-time darkness, he'd given up and decided to unpack some of Crys' old things. Maybe that would help him feel close to her again. Or maybe he'd find a clue about where she went, why she'd come back different.

The records in their milk crate. The record player. Jesse wanted to play one, even one of the ones he didn't like, but he knew that would wake up the rest of the house. He moved on to a cardboard box.

A notebook full of ballpoint pen drawings. Jesse hadn't realised Crys was so into art. The drawings were of trees, dragons and androgynous naked people. Everything was spiky and stretched out, heavily shaded. He thought inadvertently of his wet dream — the trees reminded him of it. Their branches writhed against each other in snaky, mobile braids, like they might reach out and caress the naked people, or bind them. Here and there, Crys had added a skull, a gun, a noose, a cartoonish bottle of booze with XXX on the label. Jesse wasn't sure if he liked the drawings or not, but they were pure Crys, and that gave him a tiny, painful twinge of happiness.

Another notebook, this time blank inside. Three foil-wrapped condoms fell out when Jesse picked it up.

The moth that had been hovering above a box flap moved towards him. It landed very close, perching on the rim of the box he was rifling through. Its wings were fuzzy at the edges, silver-shiny like moonlight.

The box was big, so there was a lot of stuff left in it. Jesse found Crys' headphones, a few tapes and her Walkman — really? She hadn't wanted her *Walkman*? One of the tapes was *Under the Pink,* with that Tori lady dressed all in white on the cover, surrounded by billowing, strangely folded white shapes. She reminded Jesse of the moth.

He put on the headphones, put the tape in the

Walkman and pressed the play button. Tinkly piano. The woman's high, swooping voice, full of yearning and regret. The song swelled with violins and jangled briefly with electric guitar as he kept digging. It was better than he remembered.

Jesse found, examined, and put aside a pencil case filled with pens and pencils and Sharpies, a novelty pencil sharpener shaped like a globe, a pamphlet from the Church of the Subgenius, several paperback horror novels with blood-dripping titles and stepback covers. There was a rusty pair of scissors and a stuffed rabbit with a missing eye that Crys hadn't slept with since she was younger than Jesse was now.

At the bottom of the box were a bunch of badly photocopied zines. Crys was always reading zines, so that wasn't surprising. But these weren't full of music reviews, or advertisements for fake religions like Discordianism and the Church of the Subgenius. They weren't black and white comic books full of jokes about sex and drugs and killing Republican politicians. They weren't punk rock hobos' personal diaries about train hopping from city to city. Jesse had seen Crys reading all of those in the past. She'd showed them to him, talked about them with him. She'd even given him a few to keep, whether he wanted them or not.

Jesse had never seen Crys reading any of *these*

zines. He lifted them from the box, disturbing the moth at last, and spread them out on his bed. The moth drifted back out the window and into the dark.

Some of the zines had titles like *Trans Fag Rag* and *The Transgender Community Information Monthly*. Some of them had more obscure titles, but the words and pictures on the front or the first couple of pages made it obvious that they were about the same topics.

Jesse was vaguely aware that transsexuals existed, but he didn't think he'd ever met one. What was Crys doing with these? She wasn't a man who wanted to be a woman; she was already a girl. His heart raced, and he began to really study the zines, feeling shy and scared and a little excited. Tori Amos crooned about roses and prison towers. The paper left smudgy marks on his fingertips.

Oh, Jesse thought, after a few minutes of reading. There weren't just men who wanted to be women. There were women who wanted to be men, too. There were all sorts of people who started new lives as a sex other than the one they'd been declared at birth. There were cross-dressers and people who were some third thing in between male and female, and… his head spun with it all. He felt like he had been raised not knowing what colours were and had just found out about rainbows. It was impossible for him to even picture some of the stuff described in the zines. When the zines did have pictures, he stared at them until he was sure if he looked for even one more second, he would faint or die or burst into flames or something.

He couldn't know for sure why Crys had these zines. But the more he thought about it, the more Jesse thought maybe his older sister wasn't his older sister after all.

A lot of the zines were mostly, or even entirely, about female to male transsexuals who liked other men, who lived as gay guys. The idea of being gay as something desirable, something you'd choose when you didn't *have* to be it, was weird to Jesse. Weird and kind of disturbing. It fit Crys perfectly, though. Crys had never shied away from conflict, or wanted things to be easy.

Crys. Liking boys, dating boys, never making jokes about gays or lesbians or AIDS the way most people did. Wearing her hair chin length and greasy and covering her face, like a grunge rock boy, like Kurt Cobain. Refusing makeup, dresses, girls' clothes, anything that showed she had breasts. That time she tried to get Jesse and Marcus to teach her how to pee standing up. Her desire to escape her body with any drug she could get her hands on, to cut it and change it with razors and knives. Her name — his name. Never Crystal, only Crys.

It all snapped into focus in Jesse's head, like a

magic eye picture he'd stared at in just the right way. The shape of a brother he'd never quite known.

The knowledge of just how wrong the Crystal sleeping in the bedroom beside his really was.

That couldn't be the Crys who'd disappeared, no matter what had happened during those two lost days. There was no way.

Jesse didn't care if he was being irrational. He had to do something. He had to figure out how to get the real Crys back, whether she — he — was kidnapped, brainwashed, replaced, whatever. Scenarios, most of them based on movies he'd seen or books he'd read, drifted through his head, each wilder than the last. Crys had a microchip implanted in his brain that controlled his behaviour. Crystal was Crys' secret identical twin. There was a potion that caused his sibling to switch between Crystal and Crys, like in *Dr. Jekyll and Mr. Hyde*. Pod people. Alien invasion. A humanoid robot. Something copying Crys, copying what it understood of human behaviour, being the most perfect girl it could be so nobody would get suspicious.

Jesse lay on his bed, poring over the zines, thinking these thoughts, until his eyes finally began to fall shut. He became aware that the music had stopped at some point, maybe a long time ago. There was only a low hiss in his ears. He had to talk to someone. Who could he talk to?

Who would believe any of this? Who wouldn't sneer in disgust and turn him away?

Not his parents. They couldn't know until he had real proof. Maybe they could *never* know.

He managed to get everything back in the box before he passed out. The light in his room still on, several white moths gathered at the window.

*

In the dream, there was only one moth. Jesse thought he recognised it. This time, he followed it through the trees, and the trees changed shape as he moved among them. They were tall mushrooms now. They were dead men's fingers, bloated and rotting, pointing ominously at a darkening sky. Their nails were cracked and split. Their knuckles were hairy. The ground bristled with rocks and thorn bushes, and it became very difficult to walk.

Jesse was still afraid, but he was less afraid than he'd been before. There was an excitement mixed in with the fear, closer to what he'd felt in that first dream. He wasn't sure if he was naked or clothed, or what he was wearing, or even what shape his own body was. Maybe, like the trees, it had changed. That was all right with him. He was finally getting somewhere. He would get there before the thing he feared caught him up in its talons or jaws. He just had to keep his eyes on the moth.

6

"Hello?" Jesse curled around the cordless phone, cradling it as close to himself as possible. Mom was in her studio and Crystal had gone with her to learn about glazing. Dad was at his office. Jesse was alone in the house, but he hid himself in the downstairs coat closet for an extra layer of privacy. It was dark here and cramped, and it smelled of wool and leather. Dad's snow boots poked Jesse in the spine. He didn't care; he felt safe. Almost safe.

"Hello," said an unfamiliar woman's voice. She sounded like she was probably a good singer. "May I ask who is calling?"

"It's Jesse," said Jesse. "I'm one of Lane's friends? I wanted to talk to him for a minute." He kept his voice as light and casual as he could.

"Jesse Greer?" said the woman. "Oh, I've been wanting to meet you! Your parents are lovely people, you know. Your mother and I have become quite good friends."

This was news to Jesse, although he'd be the first to admit he wasn't sociable and didn't pay much attention to what his parents did.

"Yeah," said Jesse. Then, inanely: "You're Lane's mom, right?"

Mrs. Thompson laughed. "Yes, I am. I'll go get him for you. And please, call me Dahlia."

Jesse heard her press her hand over the phone receiver, then a series of muffled sounds. The next voice he heard was Lane's.

"Jesse! I've been waiting for you to call. Well, not call, but, like, turn up or something. I think I gave you the wrong idea the other day. I wasn't trying to… you know. I'm not really like that."

"I wouldn't care if you were," said Jesse. "I mean, maybe I would have before, a little. Not now."

"Huh," said Lane, sounding very surprised. "What changed?"

"A lot. A lot of stuff." Jesse wasn't sure where to begin. "Thanks for returning the Bible," he said, instead. "Wasn't it risky to get your dad to bring it over?"

Lane snorted. "Dad is like a big, stupid dog. He'll do whatever you tell him, and he sits around doing nothing if no one's giving orders. He's not curious about *anything*."

Jesse had never heard anyone his age speak so contemptuously about a parent before, at least not about a parent who hadn't done something awful. "Your dad seems super nice," he said. "I liked him."

"You don't even know him," said Lane. "So what's going on with you? Was Crys mad that we took her…?"

"No. That's the thing. She didn't want it back. She's changed, Lane. She's changed completely. It's like she's an entirely different person."

"Teenagers often change their personalities," said Lane, as though he was an expert on the subject. "They're experimenting with different ways to exist in the world."

It was obviously something a parent or teacher had told him before, probably in those exact words.

"That's not what I *mean,*" said Jesse. "I know that. I've been living with Crys for the past eleven and a half years. I found some zines the other day that made me think I didn't know Crys as well as I thought I did. But I still knew Crys really well. The girl my parents brought home *isn't Crys*. She's *Crystal*. There's something really weird going on, she wanted to get rid of Crys' stuff and she acts nothing like Crys, and I thought I saw Crys' dead body in the woods the day we hung out together, when Crys was still missing, and maybe that could've had something to do with it, or maybe she got hypnotised or possessed or..." he stopped and took a deep breath. He knew the words had tumbled out in a garbled torrent. He had to hit pause and really think about how he was going to tell Lane this story. The snow boots were digging into his back super hard.

"You sound like a total nut job," said Lane.

"You know that, right? But I believe you, 'cause we're friends."

"We are? You do?"

"Yeah, of course. Only, I can't follow a word you're saying."

"Sorry. I'm trying to figure out how to put it. I'm scared, Lane."

Lane took a deep breath. "Listen," he said. "Meet me at the treehouse. Tell me about it there. It'll give you time to think. And it might be easier in person."

"My parents said I'm not allowed to go in the woods anymore," said Jesse. "Not since I found the dead body. The cops are investigating it, I guess."

"Really?" Lane sounded dubious. "A dead body? I haven't seen a single cop or cop car around here all week, man. Not on our street, not in the woods, not on the other side of the woods. You'd think they'd be all over. Nothing interesting ever happens in Narrowbrook. My mom hasn't said anything, either."

"I'm not lying!" Jesse snapped, then thought for a second. He too couldn't recall seeing any police officers or police cars in the neighbourhood since the incident. "Maybe my parents thought I was, though. Lying, or crazy. Maybe they didn't tell the police after all." His head hurt. Why had he assumed his parents would believe him? Why was he assuming *Lane* would believe him? What if he *was* crazy?

There was only one way to know for sure.

"Dad's not home and Mom's busy," Jesse said. "I can leave. If I'm not out for too long, I can come back without anyone noticing. I'll meet you at the treehouse and I'll explain everything. And then I want to show you where I found the body."

"Sick," said Lane. "Can't wait."

Finding the clearing where he'd seen the corpse was even more difficult than Jesse had expected. The woods were shallow and thin. From most points, as he and Lane trudged in sweaty circles over the mossy earth, he could hear cars or see small sections of rooftop and house siding through the trees. It was basically impossible to get lost, and that was the problem. He'd been lost when he found the clearing. He'd been farther into the woods than it seemed possible to go; every time he thought he might be getting close to the big oaks, he and Lane came out the other side of the forest and found themselves in a trash-strewn field by the side of the highway.

Jesse tried not to panic. He didn't want to be crazy. He didn't want the body to be real, either. He wanted a soothing, rational explanation for everything. He wanted Crys back. He didn't want to screw up his friendship with Lane. The wants marched around and around in his brain, going nowhere, getting more tired and frustrated with each circuit.

"This transvestite stuff is wild," said Lane. He was flipping through one of Crys' zines, which Jesse had brought to show him. He seemed to have no trouble reading and walking at the same time. "Or transsexual, or whatever. I guess I can see Crys as a guy. She's got kind of a guy face. She's short, though. Hey, do you think I'd look good in a dress? Like, would I look like a girl, or like a boy in a dress?"

"I don't know, Lane." Jesse could see the edge of the field again, and the highway beyond it. "We're not getting anywhere. This is stupid. Maybe I'd have to be high to find the right place again."

"Wanna go back for some weed?" Lane's voice was hopeful.

"Nah." Sweat kept running into Jesse's eyes. His shirt stuck to his back. "Let's get to the field and sit down someplace for a minute. On those old tires, or that big concrete block thing."

"Yeah, a rest sounds good. Hey, you know I still believe you even if we can't find squat?"

"Thanks." All the oaks around here looked dwarfish and shrivelled compared to what he remembered. The long grass in the field was snot-coloured, unhealthy.

"I hope there aren't ticks in here," said Lane

as they began to push through it. "Wow, this lady is so pretty. I can't imagine she was ever a man."

"You don't have to, like, narrate the magazine, Lane. I've already seen the whole thing."

Jesse heard a cracking sound and a thump behind him. Lane had fallen over something. That's what you get for reading while walking, thought Jesse. Then he rebuked himself. He was just cranky because they couldn't find the clearing. What if his friend was hurt? He turned to see.

Lane sat in the grass, which now reached his thin shoulders, looking startled but none worse for wear. He scratched at his head of wild hair and looked down. "Holy shit!"

"What is it?" Jesse started to move towards him.

"Wait, no, you might step on it!" Lane scooped something up in both hands and stood, presenting the object to Jesse. "Look!"

It was a human skull.

"Holy shit!" repeated Jesse.

There was no question that the skull was real. It was dirty in places; where it was clean, it was a yellowed ivory colour, not stark white. There were a few strands of colourless hair still stuck to the top. One of its cheekbones looked shattered and the back of the head was completely gone, caved in. "Did your foot do that? Damn."

"I don't think so," said Lane. "God, how long do you think he's been out here? Or she."

Jesse took the skull from Lane. It was lighter than he expected. A tiny spider skittered out from the cave of its braincase as he turned it over and around. A creepy feeling grew in his stomach. It couldn't be the same corpse, he reassured himself. Even in summer, it wouldn't have decayed that fast. He knew. He'd read books.

"I wonder if we can find the rest of the skeleton?" Lane was on his hands and knees now, digging through the grass. The zine he'd been reading flapped its pages in the light breeze, forgotten on a patch of dirt and trampled dandelions. "Jesse, come on! Oh my God! Check this out!"

Jesse set the skull beside the zine. He was starting to get a headache. His mouth was dry. A big truck roared past on the highway and he smelled diesel. He crouched beside Lane.

There was a black hooded sweatshirt lying in the grass. Stained and faded and torn. Draped over a scattering of bones. The tattered remains of a pair of jeans a little way beyond it. Scraps that might once have been a T-shirt, underwear.

"Fuck," said Jesse. "No. It can't be."

He touched the collar of the sweatshirt with shaking hands. He pulled it gently apart. The tag inside was still intact. Faded Sharpie initials read: CG.

"Jesse?"

"It's Crys," said Jesse. "I recognise the handwriting. It's the same dead body. It was always Crys. I don't know how, I mean, I don't know who or what's in my house right now, but it's not..." he poked through the grass and weeds around the sad pile of rag-covered bones, babbling. He didn't have it in him to make sense. Nothing about the situation made sense. The world didn't make sense anymore.

"Jesse. Are you sure?"

Jesse's hand brushed stone. He explored further with his fingers: a large rock. He lifted the rock and held it up to Lane. It was crusted with dried, flaking blood, very dark and very old. There was a symbol painted on it in ink that had faded from black to a purplish brown in the sun. Jesse tried to follow the lines of the symbol with his eyes, but it made him dizzy to look at.

"Holy *fucking* shit." Lane whistled through his teeth in a way painfully reminiscent of Crys. Jesse wanted to cry and scream and even, for a terrible moment, hit Lane. Smack the teeth and the sound right out of his freckled face.

Then it passed.

He was left feeling simultaneously hollow and heavy, and not much more.

"I'm sure," said Jesse. "Crys is dead. Crys was murdered."

"Jesse. Let me see the rock for a second." Lane

was tugging on it. Jesse's fingers seemed to have locked into place; he couldn't let go. "Come on, Jesse."

Jesse shook his head.

"Listen, man, it's important. I think I recognise that symbol."

Jesse stared in disbelief. He dropped the rock. Lane caught it. "What?!"

"Yeah. I've definitely seen this before. It's in one of my mom's old books. She has a bunch of crazy hippie witch stuff."

"No way." Jesse started shaking his head again. "We can't tell your mom about any of this. We're not telling anybody until we know what's going on."

"Who says we have to tell her? Let's go back to my place. I'll find the book and show it to you myself."

7

They planned to carry Crys' skeleton, or as much of it as they could find, back to Lane's treehouse, but they quickly realised that it would take them more than one trip. Lane suggested they move only the skull and the rock with the symbol on it for now, and come back for the rest later, maybe with adults. Jesse reluctantly agreed, though he suspected that as soon as they left the field, something would take his sibling's remains back again. They would be returned to the impossible clearing he and Lane hadn't found, or they would crumble to dust and blow away in the breeze.

He carefully extricated Crys' sweatshirt from the ribcage and arm bones it still sheltered. He wrapped Crys' skull in it and carried the resulting bundle under his arm, along with the zine Lane had dropped. Lane took the rock.

Without discussing it, the two boys arranged these things like an altar in a corner of the treehouse platform. The skull and the stone sat on the sweatshirt, facing each other like old enemies. The pile of Crys' zines and notebooks Jesse had brought to show Lane was a crumbling pillar behind them. Lane and Jesse regarded the tableau for a few moments.

"We should go in," said Lane. "Drink some soda. I'll try and find that book."

"My parents are gonna kill me," said Jesse.

"Nah. They won't." Lane touched his shoulder and squeezed it. "We're going to figure this thing out, and we're gonna make sure nobody else gets killed."

Jesse's throat constricted. He couldn't say any more.

"I'm real sorry about Crys," Lane added. His hand left Jesse's body. He started climbing down the tree, and, after another minute, Jesse followed.

Lane's parents were sitting in the kitchen with glasses of iced tea, holding hands across the table. They both looked up and smiled as Jesse and Lane entered the room.

Mr. Thompson was nice-looking in a clean, generic way, as Jesse remembered, with Lane's lanky build and curly hair. Mrs. Thompson looked much less like her son, although she had his nose and mouth. She was beautiful in a way Jesse hadn't known women could be beautiful outside of old silent movies: curvy and lush but sharp-featured, enormous tilted eyes, little hands and feet like a porcelain doll. She was wearing a flowing dress that was almost more like a robe or a toga, lots of silver bracelets and no shoes.

The kitchen was an organised clutter, bottles of mysterious liquids lining shelves and bundles of dried plants hanging from hooks on the walls and ceiling. The white and blue tile, carved in elaborate floral swirls, was spotless, and it looked expensive. Maybe antique. It was the type of tile Jesse's mom would see in a magazine picture and sigh over.

Jesse was glad he'd taken his sneakers off in the foyer, even though Lane had said he didn't have to.

"Hello, boys," Mrs. Thompson smiled. Jesse couldn't tell if she was wearing lipstick or if her lips were naturally red. Lane's were. Lane had a silent movie starlet mouth. "Jesse, your mother called while you were out. I told her you were here, visiting with Lane, and that you might stay for dinner. She's all right with that, although she would prefer you tell her where you're going in the future."

"Thanks, Mrs. — Dahlia," Jesse caught himself. "Thank you so much."

"No trouble. Neil," Mrs. Thompson patted her husband's hand, "would you pour the boys some cold drinks?"

Mr. Thompson began to rise from his chair. "We can get them ourselves," said Lane hurriedly. Jesse followed him to the refrigerator, which had several strange figures made of thread and sticks stuck to it with magnets. Lane handed him two cans of Mello Yello. The cans seemed out of place in the Thompsons' kitchen; Jesse felt like they should've been old-fashioned glass bottles with metal caps. Maybe with some calligraphic label for a brand he'd never heard of.

"Take these," said Lane. "My room's up the stairs, to your right, at the end of the hall. I gotta piss first."

Jesse nodded.

"Jesse," Mrs. Thompson called after him as he left the kitchen, "we have a rule in this house. Lane's door stays open when his friends are over, okay?"

Lane's room was almost as messy as Crys' had been, although he had way fewer books. He did have stacks of VHS tapes and his own little TV and VHS player. He had a computer, too; it took up most of his small wooden desk. There was a binder beside it. When Jesse opened the binder out of curiosity, it turned out to be full of floppy discs. Posters covered Lane's walls, most of them for movies and video games Jesse had never heard of. He recognised Freddy Krueger's striped sweater and burned leer. He recognised Sonic the Hedgehog.

Lane's handful of books all seemed to be comics or how-to manuals about video games and computer stuff. There were a few copies of something called the *Fortean Times* lying around, but none of the rest of it looked interesting. That disappointed Jesse. Maybe he could get Lane into Tolkien, or Ray Bradbury, or at least Stephen King.

Jesse sat on the edge of Lane's unmade bed and nursed his Mello Yello for a while. He felt like Lane was taking a long time, but maybe he was just tired and scared. Tired and scared could make seconds last for hours. The hall through the open door was bright and painted peach. Finally, and unexpectedly, Lane's head popped out of a door on the other end of the hall. He looked around as though to check that the coast was clear, spotted Jesse, and waved.

Jesse stared. Lane darted out, a stack of books in his arms. He ran silently to his bedroom with the knock-kneed grace of a giraffe and plunked the books down beside Jesse. His eyes were shining.

"Okay, so! Mom's gonna kill me if she finds out I took these without asking, but here are the books I might've seen that symbol in." He fanned out four slim, nearly identical volumes bound in crumbling leather. They each had a different set of symbols embossed on the front cover, but none of the symbols were the one painted on the rock. These, Jesse thought, looked more like astrological signs, or hieroglyphs. There was no title or author on any of the four book covers. When Jesse opened one, it was written in the Roman alphabet but did not appear to be in English. He squinted at the page. The dense Gothic script made it hard to tell.

"Keep an ear out for Mom and Dad coming up the stairs," said Lane. "We'll need to hide these fast if they check on us." He pushed a fifth book towards Jesse. "This one's, like, fine for me to read. Thought it might help, though."

The front cover had a woodcut illustration of a pilgrim-type woman cringing away from a goat-footed devil and a flying snakelike creature. They were surrounded by bushes and trees, implying a forest. *Folk Tales and Ghost Legends of Narrowbrook, Hallridge, and the Callum County Region,* it said above the picture. Beneath it: *Collected and re-told by Dr. Emil Fifer, Ph.D.*

"That's really specific." Jesse opened *Folk Tales and Ghost Legends* to look at the table of contents. "How many ghost stories about Callum County can there even *be*?"

Lane shrugged. "Fifer's some college professor down at State. Mom knows him. I guess this is what he's interested in. Apparently we've got more ghost stories than most places, or better documented ones, at least."

"Have you read it before?"

"I've skimmed." Lane flopped on his belly across the bed. "Look, you take that one and I'll look through these others to see if I can find the symbol. They're in Latin or something, so I dunno how we'll figure out what it *means,* but maybe there'll be a diagram. A drawing."

Jesse accepted his friend's proposition with relief. He began to read *Folk Tales and Ghost Legends,* keeping his ears open and looking up at the door every few minutes.

The first two stories were about a haunted house and a haunted coal mine, respectively, neither of which were in Narrowbrook. The third was extremely long-winded, and the gist of it was that sometimes people saw floating lights in the forest and later died in bizarre ways, unless they didn't, and that this might or might not be connected to ancient, restless spirits that dwelled in the trees and rocks around Narrowbrook. The fourth story was about another haunted house. The fifth was about a man who got lost in the woods for two days, but found that twenty years had passed when he returned to town. Jesse thought it was a pretty obvious Rip Van Winkle rip-off.

He was getting a little frustrated. Dr. Fifer's writing was often dry and clunky, and he seemed to have no sense of pacing. He kept skimming over the exciting parts of the stories, while dedicating multiple paragraphs to things like the differences between Protestant sects and how houses were built in the nineteenth century. Still, Jesse kept going. What else did he have? Maybe he and Lane would need to visit the public library later.

The sixth story was called "The Changeling", which didn't sound promising, but when Jesse read the first few paragraphs his heart surged.

In 1835, Caroline Myles disappeared into the woods for four days while collecting water from a well. She was twenty years old, and she lived with her husband and their new baby on a small farm outside of Narrowbrook, bordering what was then the massive Callum forest.

Joseph Myles feared that his wife had been devoured by wolves or bears. He avowed that she would never abandon him willingly. With this in mind, Joseph and his neighbours searched the woods looking for Caroline, or for some trace of her remains. On the fourth day, a teenage boy called Adam Whitby discovered Caroline unconscious and supine, without the bucket she'd carried into the forest or the clothes she had been wearing, cradled by the exposed roots of an enormous oak.

When roused, Caroline seemed unharmed, and Whitby helped her back to her home and her husband. But it would soon become clear to all that the young woman who returned from the woods was very different from the one who had vanished…

The story went on to describe how the returned Caroline Myles seemed to remember almost nothing of her previous life. She wouldn't acknowledge her husband or baby. She refused to do housework and regularly went to town to flirt brazenly with other men. She was cruel and prone to shouting, breaking things, and getting drunk in public. Whispers began to circulate among the people of Narrowbrook that the real Caroline Myles had been replaced with a changeling, a fairy or demon that mimicked Caroline's shape to cause mayhem.

Joseph Myles resisted the rumours at first. He was not a superstitious man. He believed it possible his wife had been driven mad by something she encountered in the woods, but held out hope she might regain her senses.

Then animals around the Myles farm started turning up dead, their throats torn open and their limbs wrenched from their bodies. Joseph sat up all night hoping to catch the animal that had killed the cat, the rooster, four chickens, and all three of his spring lambs.

When he saw his wife, naked and creeping on all fours, approach the henhouse, he fired his shotgun. He meant to hit the ground beside her and frighten her away. Instead, the bullet hit Caroline in the shoulder. She cried out in 'an inhuman voice'. As Joseph watched in horror, his wife turned towards him, her eyes glowing green in the dark. She stood up. She appeared to pluck the bullet from her arm and throw it scornfully in the dirt. Then she 'made a sound like the bark of a fox' and 'let go her bladder above the place where the bullet lay'.

Joseph fainted.

In the morning, he would find every one of his chickens slaughtered. There was a bullet lying on the muddy ground near the henhouse. Joseph's best sheep had been disembowelled and strung up from the rafters of his barn by their entrails. His baby was missing, and the baby's crib was soaked through with blood.

Caroline was missing, too, and this time no one would ever see her again.

For the rest of his days, Joseph haunted the local drinking establishments, telling anyone who would listen that his wife had been replaced by a changeling. He'd say his mistake had been to shoot at her. He should have stabbed her with something made of silver while she slept. That would have killed the changeling and, presumably, allowed the real Caroline to return.

Jesse dog-eared the first and last pages of the story. "Lane," he said, at the exact moment Lane exclaimed, "Jesse!"

"Jinx." Lane looked excited. "Guess what, I totally found the symbol. But you go first."

Jesse showed Lane the story. "Not all of it fits," he admitted. "Crystal behaves *better* than Crys ever did. She hasn't done a single crazy thing, except for waxing the floor. She definitely hasn't been running around naked and killing animals."

"But she *is* totally different," said Lane.

"Something in the woods *got* Crys and sent back a copy. That sounds like a changeling to me." He considered for a moment. "Maybe it's, like, an opposite thing? If you're good, the copy is bad, and if you're bad, the copy is good." He con-sidered for another moment. "Not that Crys was a bad person. You know what I mean."

"No," said Jesse. "I don't think whatever's out there cares about good and bad at all. I think there must be a different reason." He shuddered. "It could have learned a lot about Narrowbrook people since 1835. Maybe this is how it tries to blend in and avoid suspicion."

"Right."

"I bet it's happened more than just two times. Lane, do you remember ever hearing other stories like this? Or did you ever know another kid who disappeared? Who changed all of a sudden?"

Lane looked uneasy. He shifted on the mattress and looked nervously through the open door. "Well. Uh. Sure, there are stories. Not about changelings or werewolves or whatever, but mysterious vanishing? It's a small town near the woods. If someone runs away or goes missing, people talk about it forever." He ran both hands through his hair, pulling it into a mess of frizz.

Jesse reached for the book of symbols at Lane's side. He stopped when he heard a creaking sound — it seemed to come from the hallway. He whipped his head towards the door, but no one was there.

"Jesse." To Jesse's surprise, Lane put one of his hands gently on Jesse's chin and turned his face so that they were eye to eye. It was uncomfortable, but not unwelcome. Lane's eyelashes were so long. His eyes reminded Jesse of a giraffe, as much as his height and knobby knees did. "Jesse, listen. That's not all."

Lane took a deep breath. Jesse held his. It was clear to him that Lane was about to confess something important.

"Remember Stephen Morrow?"

Jesse nodded.

"I kind of lied to you, when we first met. I'm not sure if I'm gay or whatever, and I'm not sure if Stephen is, or was. But we did kiss a lot last winter." Lane seemed to be daring Jesse to look away from him in disgust or embarrassment. His gaze became a glare, but Jesse held it. "Only ever up here, when he was visiting after school. It started out as, like, a practice thing, because we figured we might get girlfriends in middle school. We weren't ever going to tell anyone we'd practised with each other first."

Jesse didn't speak. He didn't move or look away.

"It was fun. We both really liked it. We really liked each other. I'd never had those kinds of feelings before..." Lane shook his head and made a little huffing noise in the back of his throat. "Anyway, it got out of control, I guess. Mom came in one day to bring us a snack, and she didn't knock, and she found us. She sent Stephen home, and she called his stepmom, and she told me I couldn't have him over anymore."

"I'm really sorry. That sucks." Jesse reached out to hug Lane. It felt like what Crys would have done, like the thing he was supposed to do in this situation. Lane crushed Jesse's face against his skinny chest, but continued speaking. Jesse could feel Lane's words humming inside his body. He didn't mind the hug, he decided. It was more than kindness; he wanted to be close to this boy.

"So I figured, okay, that *does* suck, but we can still be best friends. We'll hang out at school. It'll all be fine in a year or so, like nothing ever happened." Lane sniffled, his voice caught, and Jesse realised he must be crying, or about to cry. "It didn't turn out like that, of course. When I showed up at school the next day, he was out sick. He was sick the day after that, too. And on Friday, he was just this completely different guy. Haircut, no glasses, a shirt I'd never seen him wear. Wouldn't look at me. Wouldn't talk to me. He even *moved* different."

"Are you sure it wasn't..." Jesse tried to think of a tactful way to phrase his thoughts. "I mean, that doesn't sound supernatural to me. Maybe his parents really told him off. Maybe he was ashamed." As he spoke, though, he doubted himself. He remembered meeting Stephen after he'd run screaming from the clearing in the woods. Dead looking grey eyes. Dead sounding, flatly polite voice.

"You didn't fucking know him!" snapped Lane. "I know how it sounds, Jesse. And I also know there was something super wrong about it. He wasn't just *ashamed*." Lane was definitely crying now, wetting Jesse's hair with his tears. "I believed you about Crys. I trusted you. Please believe and trust me about Stephen. I didn't have an explanation for it before. I wasn't as brave as you. I never looked for one."

"Okay." Jesse patted Lane's back. "Okay. I'm not brave, but I believe you." He brushed his lips against Lane's cheek. He wasn't sure what had possessed him to do it, but Lane didn't recoil. Not at all. He held Jesse for a minute or two, then regained some composure.

"…anyway." Lane wiped his nose with the back of his hand. "I'll show you the symbol."

It was the same symbol that had been painted on the killing rock. No question. Jesse felt nauseated looking at it; it seemed to writhe against the brittle paper it was printed on. It was a throbbing tumour set dead in the centre of the page, in a circle by itself, surrounded by text in Latin or whatever. Three thick black lines connected its circular prison to three smaller circles, which contained their own shapes. The smaller shapes were much easier to take in.

"I know what these mean," Lane pointed to the smaller shapes. "They're alchemical signs. Mom taught a few of them to me. That's silver," he indicated the one that looked like a crescent moon. "So that part fits with the story in the book. The other two are salt and blood, I think? Or maybe the second one's rust. Blood doesn't make sense if these are supposed to be the copy's weaknesses."

"I'm not going to stab Crystal with a silver knife. Salt sounds less scary, and it won't hurt her if..." *If we're wrong.* Jesse swallowed the words. "I don't want to hurt anyone. I just want the fake Crys gone. I just want to know what happened."

Lane looked as though he was about to say something, but he didn't. Both boys could hear stairs creaking under ascending feet. They didn't have much time before whoever it was entered the hallway.

Without consulting each other, Jesse and Lane both grabbed an armful of books and shoved them under Lane's bed. They rearranged Lane's drooping comforter to cover all sight of the books completely.

When Mrs. Thompson entered the room, Jesse

and Lane were standing several feet from each other, far from the bed, each trying his hardest to appear absorbed in reading the back cover copy of a different VHS tape. Jesse's was something about an evil ambulance that ran people over; he scanned the same paragraph over and over without processing it.

If Mrs. Thompson found their behaviour suspicious, she gave no indication. "Boys," she said, her voice rich and sweet, "dinner is ready. Neil cooked us a real feast."

8

Jesse had no idea if dinner was any good or not. He forked bits of potato, chicken and carrot into his mouth without tasting them. He swallowed with effort. It was all dirt, paste, nothing. He let Mr. and Mrs. Thompson's attempts at conversation fall through his ears like white noise. Lane was talking enough for both of them, putting on an exaggerated show of normalcy.

After the table was cleared, the Thompson parents made it clear that they expected Jesse to return home before it got dark. They were terribly kind about it, but in a way that left no room whatsoever for contradiction or argument. Jesse had to settle for waving goodbye to Lane from several feet away, a fake-cheerful promise that they'd see each other soon. Not tomorrow; Lane had karate lessons tomorrow and his dad was taking him to buy new sneakers. But soon.

The air felt heavy when Jesse stepped outside. The sun hadn't begun to set yet, but the sounds of night insects swirled around the Thompsons' driveway. A few stray fireflies blinked past Jesse as he walked the short distance back to his own house. A white moth accompanied him most of the way, fluttering in confused and dizzy spirals. Maybe it was attracted to his sweat, his fear, his shiny, greasy hair. He hadn't remembered to shower for several days.

A plan took shape in Jesse's mind. It wasn't a great plan, but it was a start; it was something. He hoped his family hadn't had dinner yet.

But they had. When he opened the door, his mother told him as much. She and Dad were watching the news in the living room.

In Rwanda, there was an ongoing genocide. Children were being slaughtered in the streets. In Japan, authorities were searching for the perpetrators of a poison gas attack that left eight people dead and hundreds sickened.

"You don't need to see this, Jesse," said Dad, changing the channel to a ball game.

"I'm sorry we didn't save you any casserole," said Mom. "We thought you were eating at the Thompsons'."

"I did. It's okay. Where's Crystal?"

"In the kitchen, still." Mom smiled. "She said she'd do the dishes."

On TV, tiny men in jerseys pushed and shoved at each other on a green field. They passed the ball back and forth. They moved so close to their opponents that they had to be breathing each other's breath.

The Greers had a dishwasher, but it didn't

work that well. Crystal was ignoring it. Streams of steaming tap water ran over her yellow-gloved hands as she scrubbed damp food scraps off plates. Her slim, scarless arms were a little red from the heat of the water. Her face was expressionless; her cheeks seemed to have no pores. She looked very beautiful, and all wrong.

"No thank you," she said in response to Jesse's offer of a snack. "We've just eaten. I'm full."

"You're sure you don't even want some Gatorade or something?" Jesse fought to keep his voice sounding casual. Normal.

Crystal nodded. "I'm sure." She placed a plate on the drying rack, where it sparkled like the floors did when she'd waxed them.

"Suit yourself." Jesse went to his room. He put the Tori Amos tape on the Walkman, lay in bed and closed his eyes. There would be plenty of time to put his plan into action tomorrow, he reassured himself. He could wait.

The sky got darker, but the trees got brighter. Flatter. They were like paper cut-outs of trees now, and the real trees were the massive, twisting shadows behind them. Jesse kept his eyes on the moth that flew ahead of him, untouched by the reaching branches and treacherous, jagged rocks. Sweat dripped from his hair into his eyes and he wiped it away. The air was soft and heavy. He could smell decay, and he could

smell himself. He wasn't a little boy anymore. He was going to have to start using deodorant.

Eyes on the moth. Follow the moth. Jesse did not know if following the moth would make everything all right in the end, but he knew the alternative was unendurable. Lost forever, always pursued, always about to be grasped by a terrible hand. At least this way he was doing something besides waiting for death or running away.

In the distance, Jesse could see where the trees and their shadows parted like a stage curtain. There was a deep hole in the world there: a pit that swirled with every colour, iridescent as the moth's wings. Jesse knew he was going there. He was going there to discover something important. He was going there to be swallowed up and — not killed, but changed. Forever. Maybe Crys was in there, too. Maybe Crys was alive on the other side of that shimmering hole.

The smell was horrible. Jesse was definitely naked; rivulets of sweat ran down his skin. When he looked at himself, he saw that some of the wet streaks were blood. He didn't remember clearly when he'd gotten all these cuts and scrapes, but they didn't alarm him too much. He had to be okay with blood. That was important, he knew. He had to be okay with all the different juices and secretions a human body could produce. He would need it on the other side of the hole, when he finally left the forest. When he learned what the moth wanted him to learn.

Jesse thought he heard someone call his name. He looked up, but the moth was silent and hovering.

The call came again, and he turned to look behind him. There was someone else on the path. A human figure wrapped in shadows with shining eyes.

Jesse woke up before he realised who it was.

*

Jesse stood in front of the pottery shed, psyching himself up to enter. He couldn't wait long, or the tomato and mayonnaise sandwiches would get soggy. Mom's voice sounded from inside the shed, then Crystal's. The whirr of the wheel. Mom's voice again.

The paper plate balanced on Jesse's right hand held an ordinary tomato and mayonnaise sandwich. The paper plate on his left hand held an identical sandwich, but one with a thick layer of table salt hidden between the bread and the tomato on the bottom side. Jesse hoped one bite would be enough for the salt to do whatever it did.

Jesse took a long breath. "Lunch is ready!" he called at the closed door of the little stone building. Almost immediately, Crystal opened it. She was wearing some of her old, shapeless clothes again, but only so they would get messy. There were smears and splotches of grey clay across her chest and thighs. Her hair fell silkily from a high ponytail. She still had on lip gloss.

"Here." Jesse handed her the plate in his left hand. She took it without saying anything and stared down at the sandwich.

Jesse's mom approached. Her palms dripped with water and there was a sharp line between the dried clay on her forearms and the clean skin of her freshly washed hands.

"Thank you, Jesse." She took her plate and, still standing, bit into the sandwich. "Mmm! I'm going to finish this outside. It's such a beautiful day."

Crystal was still standing by the door. She picked at the crust of her sandwich with her fingers, but made no move to eat.

"You've gotta be hungry, Crystal," said Jesse.

Crystal shook her head.

"Come on," he tried, "I know you didn't have breakfast. I made these sandwiches special. They're so good."

"They are delicious," Mom agreed. "What's in them?"

"Wheat bread, mayonnaise, the first tomatoes from Dad's garden. Some dill. I didn't use any salt or pepper," said Jesse. "I know you're trying to cut down your sodium intake."

"With tomatoes this fresh, you don't need salt," said Mom. "Or pepper." She looked at Crystal. "You should have at least one bite, sweetheart. Don't hurt your brother's feelings."

Crystal's eyes were a grey cipher. She lifted the sandwich the way she might have picked up a plastic bag of dog shit. Jesse held his breath.

Crystal bit off a tiny corner. Chewed. Swallowed. Stopped. Looked curiously at the sandwich in her hands.

She took a bigger, more enthusiastic bite. Jesse was trembling with adrenaline. She had definitely just gotten a mouthful of salt; even if it didn't make her shrivel up like a slug, or turn into a demon or something, she was about to start gagging and spitting and choking. Maybe getting mad at him, although he couldn't really picture what she'd look like mad. Nothing like Crys, he was sure.

But nothing happened. Nothing except for loud chewing and swallowing as Crystal polished off the entire sandwich in thirty seconds, with every appearance of enjoyment and a lack of manners that made her seem more like Crys than she ever had since returning with their parents. Was she mocking him? Did she know what he'd meant to do?

"My!" said Mom, a little taken aback.

"Glad you both liked them," muttered Jesse. Time to retreat and regroup. "I'd better get back to the house."

Mom and Crystal both came out of the shed after him. Jesse was almost sure they could hear his heart beating, loud and fast.

When Mom walked ahead to the backyard picnic table, Crystal grabbed Jesse's arm. Her hands felt almost cold enough to burn. Her grip was steel or stone or iron.

"You. Meet me in my bedroom in ten minutes," she whispered into his ear. "I know you know. I'll explain everything. Be there."

9

Jesse stood in the middle of Crystal's empty bedroom floor preparing himself for a fight. Or, at the very least, a confrontation of some kind. Threats. Crystal's room smelled faintly metallic. He balled and relaxed his fists several times. He stared at the hospital corners on her neatly made bed. It was better than staring at the door, waiting for it to open.

He shivered, startled, when it finally did.

Instead of angry, Crystal looked scared and sick. Her eyes were wild and they seemed to shift from grey to black and back again, over and over. Her face was shiny with sweat. A strand of spit glistened at the corner of her mouth.

"I don't have much time, human boy," she said. Her voice was nothing like Crys' now, and it wasn't docile and flat, either. It growled and rumbled and creaked. "You need to listen to me. We can help each other, but you must do exactly as I say."

"I don't need your *help*." Jesse's hands were fists again. "And you don't need mine. You're invading my family and I want you to *get out now*. Out of this house. Out of our lives. I'll call Mom, I'll show her what you really are—"

A hideous grinding noise cut him off, like rocks rolling over each other down a steep slope. Maybe it was the Crystal-thing's laughter. "Oh, your mother knows exactly what I am. She helped put me in this body."

Jesse goggled at her. "What? No."

"We covet physical bodies. We covet lives. We have none of our own. Sometimes we can steal the life and the shape of a lost hunter, a starving child, a drowned girl. We can use the shape to get more life. It used to be much easier, but the woods in your world are small these days, and we are very weak." Crystal paused and licked her lips. She sucked the strand of spit back through her teeth. "Cunning men and women know that. They can lure us with a sacrifice, laid open like a gift. We can't resist the trap. And when we've slurped up that life and taken that shape, we find ourselves bound by their sigils. The fetishes they put inside us while we're still changing form."

"Fetishes?" Jesse thought of men masturbating into high-heeled shoes. "Listen, I know my parents aren't witches or Satanists or whatever. They're nice people. They would never sacrifice anybody, let alone their *own kid*. I don't believe that."

"Your parents are very nice people," agreed Crystal. "And they are not witches. They had help. The sacrifice itself was incidental to them, you see. I'm sure they found it unfortunate. What they wanted was a daughter they could control. The eldest child they felt they deserved. Someone happy and good and ordinary."

"But the real Crys is *dead*! And you're not any of those things!"

Crystal smiled. It was a smile Jesse had never seen before. It was much worse than her laugh. She walked over to the bed and sat down on it, patting the space beside her in invitation.

Jesse didn't move.

"Suit yourself. I've been around a long time, human boy. I've seen a lot of your kind come and go through my woods. I can tell you true: nice people don't care about what things *are*. They care about how things *seem*."

"*I'm* nice," Jesse protested. "At least, I think so."

"You put salt in my sandwich, human boy." Another grinding avalanche rumble. "So much salt. Were I human, it would have pickled my tongue."

Jesse was at a loss. He tried to picture his parents killing Crys, or giving permission for Crys to be killed; he couldn't. It was even harder and worse to imagine than his parents trucking Crys off to an insane asylum or a boot camp.

But. A worm of doubt in his brain. He remembered standing with Crys on the porch. A solstice sunset that felt very long ago now. *Mom and Dad are at their wit's end, I guess. They think nothing they do is going to change me or fix me.*

Mom and Dad never cared if Crys' medication made Crys feel bad, only if it made Crys act calmer. They hated all of Crys' friends and boyfriends. They hated everything Crys wanted to do, even if it was harmless, unless it was something they also wanted Crys to do.

They're nice people, but I'm a terrible daughter. I'm the worst daughter in the world.

Jesse couldn't imagine they would have let Crys get a sex change, or even talk about wanting one, or go out and live as a boy, with a boy's name and a bound chest and underwear stuffed with socks. He couldn't imagine that they would even accept it if one of their children turned out to be gay. They'd be nice about it, of course. They wouldn't kick him out or anything. But…

"What do you want me to do?" asked Jesse, suspicion heavy in his mouth. "And how do you think you can help me?"

Crystal's eyes turned grey, then black, then grey again. A silver shimmer rippled across them. "I can only speak freely now," she said. "My movement is still limited and my powers are bound by the fetish. Find something silver. A brooch pin, a blade, a coin. It needn't be sharp. Come back to my room tonight and cut the fetish from my chest with it. Do it, and I can promise that neither I nor any of my kind will ever hurt you in these woods."

"What if I just kill you with the silver instead? It can kill you, right?"

"You don't know the first thing about what can kill me, human whelp." The horrible smile was back. "Understand? A cut is no injury to me."

Jesse gulped. His legs swam beneath him. "What's a fetish? I mean, what does it look like?"

"It's an object of power. A little charm made of things that belonged to your sister and some type of spell-writing. Magic symbols. It will be," Crystal tapped the space between her breasts, "in here, beneath the outer layer of flesh."

"Fuck," said Jesse. "Okay. But *fuck*."

"You'll do it, then." Crystal's black eyes narrowed. "Yes. I think you will do it, human boy." She stood from the bed and lurched for the door, as though on a pitching ship at sea. "I need to go to your mother now. The salt is dissolving."

Jesse watched her ponytail bob away as she descended the stairs. The back of her neck looked clammy and her skin inhumanly pale. Her hands shook.

When she turned a corner and he couldn't see her anymore, he sat down where Crys had kept the record player and sobbed.

10

The only thing in the house Jesse was sure was made of silver was a set of cutlery that his parents had gotten as a wedding present. Mom claimed it was being saved for special occasions. Jesse couldn't remember ever using the utensils, or seeing them used, but he knew where they were kept.

He waited until after midnight, when he was sure his parents would be asleep. The numbers on his clock dawdled as he watched white moths fly in and out the window. He listened to Tori Amos scream-singing that she believed in peace. It wasn't hard to keep himself awake.

It was hard to force himself to get out of bed and creep downstairs. It was hard to push a chair over to the bank of cabinets lining the wall behind the stove without making noise. It was hard to decide, after finding the silver cutlery wrapped in linen in one of the uppermost cabinets, what to take.

There were only butter knives and regular table knives. None of them looked sharp at all. Jesse briefly considered using one of the big forks as an alternative, then decided that was stupid. He took a silver knife and tried as best he could to conceal it along the underside of his arm. He put the rest back as he'd found them and replaced the chair.

The refrigerator hummed in the dark of the house. Jesse could hear water gurgling through pipes inside the walls. His own breathing and movements seemed very, very loud. Next came the hardest part of all.

Jesse walked upstairs as if in slow motion. He froze and held his breath each time he accidentally stepped on a squeaky part of the floor.

He opened the door to Crys' room. Crystal had left the windows open. Some more of the white moths fluttered crazily around a glowing lamp; Crystal had taken it from its usual place on her dresser and set it beside the bed. Jesse wasn't sure if he was grateful for the light or not, if the gesture was even meant as a kindness to him or not.

Crystal lay on her back, above the bedcovers. Her eyes were closed. The rise and fall of her chest was gentle and even. She wore a white, slip-like nightgown Jesse had never seen before. The topography of her body beneath the satin made him uncomfortable.

Jesse stood beside Crystal. Lifted the knife above the smooth skin of her chest where he was supposed to stab. He worried he wouldn't be able to do it. He doubted, again, whether his parents could ever really have looked at Crys, the real Crys, vulnerable and helpless in the long grass, and brought a rock down upon their own child's skull.

He worried he was being tricked in some way he couldn't yet understand.

He didn't see that he had any real options in this situation. There was one way forward, and he had to take it. Time would go on with or without his action. Crys would still be dead. Crys would still be dead.

Jesse brought the silver knife's dull blade down. He did it as hard as he could, still half-expecting it would slip off leaving only a bruise. Fully expecting resistance, at least.

Instead, he fell forward onto Crystal's hard, cold body as the knife tore through her flesh like it was wet silk. Dark blood oozed out of the hole it made, staining the white nightgown, staining him.

Crystal made a gasping sound and sat up, her hands clawing at Jesse's back.

He grabbed the knife again, fingers slipping on the handle, and tugged clumsily. Crystal tore open: he could see fat and muscle peeling away on both sides of the slit, and though she bled a lot, it was a strange, syrupy blood. There wasn't as much of it as there should have been. It smelled like something left by the side of the road to rot in high summer.

Crystal's mouth opened and closed like the

mouth of a fish about to be gutted. Drowning in air. Jesse went fishing with an uncle once; he'd hated it.

Another inexpert slash with the knife. She was pulling his hair, her legs were kicking. He tried not to let her crush his face into her heaving chest. He let the knife drop and pushed into the hole he'd made with both sticky hands. Crystal kept writhing, but didn't try to stop him.

Inside Crystal's body, past the outer layers of flesh, there was bone and there was rancid-smelling blood. There were no organs Jesse could recognise. She was a hollow vessel filled with soup, an open sewer.

He rummaged through the awful liquid, feeling for anything not rib-like to grab hold of. He breathed heavily through his mouth. When he inhaled through his nose by accident, he retched. Nearly vomited. Crystal's hands were beating a weak drum on his back. He felt the other side of her. The spine.

He moved his hand down. Down. *There*. Tethered between vertebrae. Like a swollen, sodden chrysalis.

Jesse pulled at the object. Blood sloshed. It resisted, and resisted, then came away in his hand with a squelching noise.

Crystal seized. Her back arched, spilling more blood onto the bed and throwing Jesse off her. He fell to the floor, the wet object heavy in his clenched fist, and rolled into the lamp and knocked it over; Crystal was mostly out of the light now, and Jesse was glad he couldn't see her face.

He opened his hand. It was a fabric wrapped lump, clotted hair stuck out of one end. It could have been fabric from Crys' sweatshirt, hair torn from Crys' scalp. It could have been fabric from anywhere, hair from anyone. The symbol from the rock was scrawled on it in something white and apparently blood proof. It shone for a moment, then dimmed and died. Looking at it made Jesse feel nauseated and dizzy.

He dropped the fetish on the floor and looked away.

Crystal stood shakily from the bed. She knelt beside Jesse. There wasn't a hole in her chest anymore. When she smiled at him, she had more teeth and they were sharper. Other than that, she looked the same.

Her nightgown was ruined, stained with gore all down the front. A clot of gelatinous bloody material hung from its low neckline like a pendant.

Crystal grabbed two moths from the air and shoved them in her mouth. She swallowed them whole, then grinned even wider.

"Starving. I'm going to need more."

Jesse scrambled backwards. "You promised you wouldn't hurt me."

She laughed her stone-grinding laugh. "Don't worry, little one. I don't intend to. Your *parents,* on the other hand... well, I think they ought to pay for what they've done." Crystal stood again and stretched like she was rising from a long nap. She cracked her toes.

Jesse retched. Nothing came up. The bad smell of Crystal's blood was, if anything, getting stronger. "Please," he croaked. "You said you'd owe me a favour. Don't hurt my parents. You said they had help. Go after that person, or those people. Leave my mom and dad alone."

"Fine." Crystal's tone was impossible to read. "A waste of a favour. But very well. I'll leave this house, then. I'll free my siblings and we will have our revenge." She picked up the silver knife and held it like a dagger. "Follow me, if you like. You might learn something."

Crystal was out the door and halfway down the stairs in a silent rush before Jesse had time to get up. He turned off the lamp and stood trembling for a moment before he did the only thing he could think to do next. He went after her.

11

By the time Jesse had pulled on his sneakers over bare feet and rushed out into the front yard, Crystal was almost past the Thompsons' house. Of course, as fast as he'd seen her move in Crys' bedroom, this was probably a leisurely strolling pace for her. Maybe she was allowing him to catch up. Maybe she was just enjoying the night air.

Jesse expected Crystal to continue down the street, towards the Morrows'. But it didn't really surprise him when she turned into the Thompsons' side yard and walked around the back of their house. Jesse wasn't a fool.

"The front door is locked," Crystal explained when Jesse caught up with her. She rattled the handle of the back door. "This one, too."

She handed Jesse the knife, then wedged her fingers and toes into cracks in the bricks of the Thompsons' house and spidered along the back wall. "Aha!" She'd found an open window on the second floor. It wasn't open wide, but she slithered through the gap with ease and disappeared into the darkness.

The moment stretched interminably. Anticipation pulsed in the air, intertwining with the night songs of cicadas and crickets. A firefly winked past Jesse's nose. He clutched the knife, white-knuckled. Should he make a run for it while Crystal was inside? When she came downstairs to the door, should he give her the knife and *then* run? He should run at some point soon, anyway. But where would he go?

An owl screamed in the woods somewhere. Lane was asleep in his bed, Jesse thought. Lane had no idea what was happening. Surely Lane had no idea what was happening.

Crystal opened the back door. It made a soft swishing sound. She held out her hand, blood-smeared palm up, like a queen.

Jesse dutifully deposited the knife there.

She turned on her heels and stalked through the kitchen and up the stairs. Jesse followed, although she never looked back to see if he was still there, or spoke to him again.

They peered into every doorway they passed. There was the silent bathroom. There was a room full of books, tchotchkes, and more bottles of strange things like the ones in the kitchen. Then a guest room with a fold-out futon and not much else in it. Jesse could have shown Crystal where to go, but he wanted to stall. He could feel violence shimmering in the near future, and it filled him with dread. Even if the violence would be against someone who, by the sound of things, richly deserved it.

She was Lane's mother, after all. Jesse felt wrong-footed, small and lost: how could their mothers, who loved them, be such awful people? People who sacrificed others' lives for the sake of order and propriety?

Finally, Crystal turned the brass doorknob to the room right before Lane's in the hallway. The master bedroom.

This door creaked as it opened, and Jesse knew, he just *knew*, the sound would wake someone this time. He covered his ears and closed his eyes.

There was a rustling noise. A grunt of surprise. A burst of something that wasn't quite light on the other side of his eyelids. It made his teeth hurt. Jesse had to look.

Mrs. Thompson was sitting up in bed, her eyes wide open and both hands extended in front of her. She was shaking a little, and her bared teeth ground against each other. Her entire body glowed like a firefly, golden-green. Beside her, Mr. Thompson lay on his back, hands folded over his chest, apparently still asleep. Crystal had stopped at the foot of the bed; she darted from side to side but seemed unable to come closer to the couple. She made a few frustrated feints at the air with the knife.

"You can't keep that up for long," she said. "It's taking a toll on you already. You're not good at shielding."

"I haven't had to in a long time," said Mrs. Thompson, through her teeth. "But I never forgot how." Then she said a few words in a language Jesse didn't know.

"That won't work on me," said Crystal. "Not now." She sidled around the bed to stand closer to Mr. Thompson. "If you drop his half of the shield, it'll be easier for you. You might live."

Mrs. Thompson grunted. "I'm not that stupid." She looked past Crystal and saw Jesse. "I should've known. I had a feeling about you. Your whole family, really. I almost told your mother no, when she asked me. My gut understood there'd be trouble." She was sweating now and her skin looked too pale beneath the firefly glow. Her hair stuck out like it was full of static electricity. She looked very beautiful anyway. Crystal was a goblin by comparison, a monster in bloody rags.

"My mother asked you," Jesse muttered. Mrs. Thompson didn't respond, and he figured he hadn't spoken loud enough for her to hear. He realised, to his own surprise, that he wanted Crystal to win this fight. He wanted, in that moment, to see her stab Mrs. Thompson, or bite her, eat her, rip her head off.

Crystal was still standing ineffectually on Mr. Thompson's side of the bed. She couldn't pass whatever invisible barrier Mrs. Thompson was generating — but maybe someone, or something, else could. Jesse looked around the room. It was too dark to make out a lot of detail, but he noticed a seashell-shaped bottle sitting on a little table within arm's reach. It was by itself, planted on a doily. Maybe perfume. Maybe something else.

Jesse grabbed the bottle. He didn't think about what he was doing. He hurled it at Mrs. Thompson.

It hit her square in the forehead, the stopper separating from the rest of the bottle, and she jerked backwards hard. A smell of honey and brine drenched the room as the liquid sprayed across the bed.

The glow around Mrs. Thompson flared, then flickered, then died. She started to sit up, cursing, making gestures with her hands, but Crystal had already seized her moment and leapt upon Mr. Thompson like a cat. She slammed the knife into his chest with confidence and precision, not minding the spray of rotten blood. Dipped her arm into the resulting hole and pulled something out, then hurled it away.

It landed at Jesse's feet. While the fetish in Crystal's chest had been recognizable as something made of cloth and paint and hair, this one was an undifferentiated, jellylike lump of decayed garbage. It might have been anything: a wad of mouldy bread, a tumour.

It must have been very old, thought Jesse.

Years old. Maybe even decades. Was Lane the son of the original Mr. Thompson, or of this creature? What would that make Lane?

Mr. Thompson screamed. His back arched; his hands clawed at nothing. Mrs. Thompson was out of bed, on her knees, trying to grab Mr. Thompson's fetish. Jesse kicked it away from her groping hands.

"You have no idea what you're messing with," Mrs. Thompson snarled. "Little bastard. You'll get half the town killed, is that what you want?!"

Mr. Thompson grabbed her by the hair and yanked her backwards. He, like Crystal, was changing. His face was no longer pleasant. His eyes were no longer empty.

"Thank you, Jesse Greer," he said in a voice like wind blowing over the top of a glass bottle. He threw his wife back onto the bed and plunged his teeth into her throat. Blood oozed from the wound, and Mrs. Thompson howled. She tried to hit him, but Crystal grabbed both her arms and wrenched them away. Jesse heard a loud *pop,* as though one or both joints had come out of their sockets.

Jesse was frozen. He didn't want to see this after all. There was nothing satisfying about Mrs. Thompson's pain. But he couldn't look away, couldn't move. Crystal had bent over and begun to chew off one of Mrs. Thompson's ears.

"Jesse?" A soft touch on Jesse's spine. He was suddenly in his body again and capable of movement; he shrieked and whirled around.

Lane stood beside him in a t-shirt and boxers, looking sleepy and worried. "Why are you here, Jesse? What's happening? Thought I heard Mom and Dad yelling..." he squinted into the dark bedroom and his eyes widened. "No. Oh, no. Dad! Stop!" He took a step forward, wringing his hands. "*Dad*! You're *hurting* her!"

Mr. Thompson smiled. "It's okay, son," he said, in a terrible parody of his former genial voice. There was a shred of flesh caught between his teeth. Blood dripped off his lower lip like syrup. "You're just having a bad dream. You should go back to bed. We'll talk in the morning."

"La–ne," moaned Mrs. Thompson, her voice gurgling and choking through her torn throat. "Lane, run. Get out."

"Mom?" Lane seemed bewildered, almost in shock. "Am I dreaming? Why does it stink in here?"

Crystal picked up the perfume bottle and smashed it into the side of Mrs. Thompson's head. It made a crunching, mushy sound.

"Run," repeated Mrs. Thompson, barely audible.

Mr. Thompson tore out a huge chunk of her neck with his teeth and chewed it with relish.

Crystal brought the perfume bottle down on Mrs. Thompson's skull again and again. The glass dripped. Mrs. Thompson's scalp started to slide out of place like a wig.

Lane seemed frozen now, and Jesse could watch no more. He grabbed his friend by the arm.

"Come on," he said, "we've got to go."

He couldn't imagine *where* they'd go, or what they'd do, but he had to keep Lane safe. Lane was all he had now. He couldn't go back to his parents, knowing what he knew. He couldn't watch Crystal and Mr. Thompson and Stephen Morrow and however many others there were eat people all over Narrowbrook, even if some of them maybe deserved it. He never wanted to see Narrowbrook again. He wished he'd never come here.

If he hadn't come here, Crys would still be alive, he wouldn't have met Lane. Lane, who was crying silently but letting Jesse lead him back to his own room, letting Jesse help him into some jeans, letting Jesse pull him downstairs.

The noises from the bedroom were indescribable, but Lane, somehow, had enough presence of mind to find where his mom had stored $500 of emergency cash behind the false back of a kitchen cabinet and take it. "Bus tickets," he explained in a hollow, panicked voice. "We can go to the Greyhound station. It's like three miles away." His eyes looked like black holes in the shadows of the kitchen. Jesse tried not to think of what Lane might or might not be. It was frightening how collected he seemed, given the circumstances. But he'd trusted Jesse; Jesse would have to trust him.

Jesse squeezed his friend's hand.

"Crystal said she wouldn't hurt me," he whispered. "I think that applies to the rest of them, too, but I'm not sure."

"What?"

"I'll explain on the way. I need to get something first, though. Can you grab a backpack or something?"

"Yeah…"

"Do it. We'll swing by your treehouse on the way out." It was probably a bad idea to go into the woods. Jesse thought, with a shiver, of all the bones that might be hidden just below the topsoil.

But he couldn't leave Crys behind.

12

The boys ran on Narrowbrook's nighttime sidewalks until their sides ached. No one was out but the nocturnal animals. They startled a possum and it hissed at them. The streetlights were yellow and rare.

When Jesse knew he could run no further, and when he was sure — pretty sure — they weren't being watched or followed, he sat down on the curb for a moment. Lane, who was in better shape, stopped when he realised he was running alone. He doubled back and crouched on his heels beside Jesse.

"Shit. You owe me an explanation. Where are we gonna go? How are we gonna survive? We're not old enough to get jobs! What if the cops come after us? What happened to your parents? Why can't *they* help?" Lane's eyes glittered in the yellow light. Tears. His whole face was wet with sweat and tears. Jesse figured his own face was, too. Maybe Lane was human after all.

"We'll get tickets to the city," Jesse said, through wheezing gasps. "How far is the bus station now?"

"Not too far. We'll have to cross the highway, though. And we'll have to wait for it to open. *Shit*."

"Okay, okay. So we'll hide somewhere until morning, then go up to the city. Crys had this friend, Marcus. He'd probably let us crash with him, I guess. If not him, maybe someone else he knows."

Lane looked doubtful. "You know I've never left Narrowbrook? Not in my whole life."

"I'm sorry. I'm so sorry. I promise I'll tell you everything that happened later. When we're on the bus. I really will."

"I never wanted to leave."

Jesse closed his eyes. Kaleidoscope patterns swam in the darkness that spread before him. He thought about Crys sneaking through the dark, trying to get away. It should've been Crys out here, with headphones on, flying home with ears full of music.

He shifted so that he felt the weight of the small backpack more firmly across his shoulder blades. There were a couple of zines in it. There was a skull wrapped in a dirty sweatshirt.

A white moth was circling the street light above them. Jesse stood up. "I'm sorry," he said again.

Everything was shadow in the forest again. Everything but the white moth and the hole in the world up ahead and Lane, who was walking beside him. Lane was naked, too, and glowing like a firefly. It was difficult to make out all of his features, but Jesse

recognised the coils of his hair, the curves of his lips, the length of his arms and legs. His eyes were full of light. The trees recoiled from him. The ground did, too. He looked like he was floating.

Jesse wondered if they were both floating. He no longer felt the stones beneath his feet.

The hole loomed before them. A wind blew out from it like a breath. It smelled of earth and gasoline. It made the sound of highway traffic. The great secret Jesse had been waiting to learn was about to be revealed. He wanted to say something to Lane, but the wind stole his words away.

The hole beckoned them closer, folded them in. Lane seemed to be laughing, or maybe screaming. Jesse felt a moment of gut-flipping doubt right as he was lifted by a powerful current of air and swept through the aperture–

Jesse woke up with the sunrise. He and Lane had slept behind the dumpster of the convenience store next to the bus station. Jesse had slept, anyway. Lane was awake, with dark rings around his eyes. The pink sky behind him looked infected. The air was already moist and heavy. Jesse smelled garbage and smoke.

"Hey," said Lane in a hoarse voice.

"Hey," said Jesse.

Sirens. A fire truck, or an ambulance, or a cop car screamed by on the road. Then another one. There was something upsetting about being able to hear but not see them.

"They open in probably an hour? Maybe two," said Lane. "I don't have a watch. I don't know."

Jesse nodded.

"There were more sirens earlier."

Jesse nodded again. They sat in silence for a while as the sky turned blue. Jesse held the backpack in his lap. He felt the shapes inside it. He thought about the things he'd have to carry for the rest of his life now. He thought about the sound of a skull smashing, and he resisted the urge to open the backpack and unwrap the grimy, tattered sweatshirt and see what was there.

He thought about how Lane might look sitting on the bus beside him, sometime later in the day, watching out the window as rivers, fields and strip malls blurred past, as he was carried to places he'd never been or wanted to go.

He thought about whether Lane was tied to the woods of Narrowbrook by some magic of his birth, whether leaving might change him or hurt him. Whether it might change or hurt him more than life already had, and would.

"Lane," said Jesse. Lane turned to him.

Jesse wanted to ask Lane if he'd forgive him. What came out instead was, "Thank you."

Jesse inhaled and looked at the newly risen sun. "I'm going to tell you everything now," he said. "I have to tell someone."

Lane leaned against him and put his hand on the backpack. Near to Jesse's, but not quite touching.

More smoke smell, more sirens. Something terrible was happening behind them. Something terrible already had.

"I'm listening," said Lane. "I'm ready."

ACKNOWLEDGEMENTS

I'd like to thank my friend Bryan Cebulski for going over an early draft of this novella and providing insightful notes, criticism, and commentary.

Thanks to my partner, Flann, for being patient and flexible while I try to make this whole "being a writer" thing work.

Thanks to R.L. Stine and Tim Jacobus for helping to start me down this path back in the 1990s.

Thanks to Nathaniel Kunitsky for editing and publishing this book, and to Sadia Bies for creating a beautiful, eerie book cover.

And thanks to you, for reading *The False Sister*.

ABOUT THE AUTHOR

Briar Ripley Page (he/they) is the author of several novellas and short stories. His other books include *Corrupted Vessels* and *Travelers' Tales.* Originally from Appalachia, Briar currently lives in London with his spouse and two horrible cats. In addition to writing, Briar has been a janitor, a hotel maid, a dishwasher, a waiter, a receptionist, an illustrator, a sandwich artist, a day camp supervisor, a dog sitter, and a full-time crazy person. He prefers carbonated beverages and dislikes crowds. His favourite colour is orange.

THE CREDITS

Creating a book is a massive team effort. Knight Errant and Briar Ripley Page would like to thank everyone who worked behind the scenes to make *The False Sister* happen.

Managing Director and Editor

Nathaniel Kunitsky

Publishing Assistant

Friday Schoemaker

Creative Director

Lenka Murová

Project Assistant

Angelica Curzi

Cover Art Illustrator

Sadia Bies

A special thank you to every single person who backed and shared our Kickstarter campaign.

Without your support our 2023 list would not have been possible.

m. turner j. hudson gabriella b. page e. morrison julie l. penland l. kraus e. bowers
o. whitney h. duncan e. claybaugh friday lindz e. reed andreas p. casey y. mittal k. sietel
brigh w. mamuna k. allen k. vikings c. page l. o'brien c. wair a. stanback b. hughes r. novak
c. cox p. kimble m. otto elena noel e. r. craig d. skea i. g. morris e. pitner dpn marina
d. psmith c. barron j. bottles i. birman j. thompson k. blair s. mayer a. penland f. rossero
dlhalp s. lloyd o. pinchuk h. mcdaid m. paley c. lewis k. lennon C r. rush-morgan vince
j. l. smith w. hughes n. hardy a. mcquaid eris anna caith zaraegis s. dunlop b. cebulski
syksy r. jones g. gregory f. ostby Creative Scotland c. donaldson j. cooper h. hirst
r. mccleary c. alexandersson sara r. vance a. jehangir daniil b. norton ophelia j. alexander
l. burwitz d. malcom k. hunziker j. oui k. turner d. carol alexandra sian gareth s. jones
fitakaleerie j. q. peterson karen rós k. CM r. page claire a. frank a. traphagan missy cara
PG m. piper a. treacy d. penland n. briggs ninedin a. grunwald p. carroll jake a. vaughn
morgan holly f. daoinsidhe c. post p. sterk Argonaut Books e. thompson sam
g. felker-martin kimberly m.p. deutsch t. orosz connie c. brienne s. mcphail g. bard
s. ingram e. van doren rxbin ian r. heafield p. stanton s. mckinlay r. rusak r. tonks j. bay
sophie d. b. moose patience n. williams c. withers áine s. cole harriet j. cole s. pybus dokja
m. noone isabela k. guilliams j. tövissy MW anna a. anderson tenille adam shana i. m. leigh
l. croal el s. smalley bethany idontfindyouthatinteresting m. huxley p. strömberg t. wymore
t. bridges c. luca l. bradley l. burns n. queen r. lindstrom p. herterich a. r. cardno p. reitz
g. casillas s. kollman b. weiss k. macaskill-smith s. norman c. j. gibson k. frey simon c.
e. davidson rayanroar n. novak midnightmare s. fraser c. spann tania c. morton j. cleak
rachlette m. young l. kapusta j. osborne k. lovick scarlet g. mitchell l. benson j. curtis
rachel owlglass i. sheene

OTHER WORK BY BRIAR RIPLEY PAGE

Corrupted Vessels (reprint from tRaum books, 2023)

Body After Body

Girls Online in the Late 2000s

More of Briar's work can be found on his personal website: : www.briarripleypage.xyz

OTHER WORK BY KNIGHT ERRANT PRESS

F, M or Other: Quarrels with the Gender Binary

Queering the Map of Glasgow

Vicky Romeo Plus Joolz by Ely Percy

Love, Pan-Fried by Gray Crosbie

Tamlin by Aven Wildsmith

The False Sister by Briar Ripley Page

Andrion by Alex Penland

The Child of Hameln by Max Turner